# ACT OF
# TREACHERY

Also by John Bishop

ACT OF MURDER

ACT OF DECEPTION

ACT OF REVENGE

ACT OF NEGLIGENCE

ACT OF FATE

ACT OF ATONEMENT

ACT OF MERCY

ACT OF AVARICE

ACT OF AGGRESSION

# ACT OF TREACHERY

## A DOC BRADY MYSTERY

# John Bishop, MD

MANTID PRESS

Act of Treachery

**A Doc Brady Mystery**

For information about this title, contact:
Attention: Permissions Department
legalquestions@codedenver.com

# CONTENTS

1. SHERIFF JOAN WILCOX . . . . . . . . . . . . . . . . . 11

2. MARY LOUISE . . . . . . . . . . . . . . . . . . . . . 17

3. THE VICTIMS . . . . . . . . . . . . . . . . . . . . . 26

4. THE RUNNER . . . . . . . . . . . . . . . . . . . . . 33

5. MONDAY, MONDAY . . . . . . . . . . . . . . . . . . 39

6. BOB JACKSON . . . . . . . . . . . . . . . . . . . . . 48

7. THE FOURTH VICTIM . . . . . . . . . . . . . . . . . 55

8. THE FBI ARRIVES . . . . . . . . . . . . . . . . . . . 62

9. INTERVIEWS, PART 1 . . . . . . . . . . . . . . . . . 71

10. PARTY . . . . . . . . . . . . . . . . . . . . . . . . . 78

11. INTERVIEWS, PART 2 . . . . . . . . . . . . . . . . . 87

12. MEDICATION RESEARCH . . . . . . . . . . . . . . . 95

13. DAY JOB . . . . . . . . . . . . . . . . . . . . . . . . 102

14. THE BADGE . . . . . . . . . . . . . . . . . . . . . . 111

15. BLUE LAKE . . . . . . . . . . . . . . . . . . . . . . 116

16. HOSPITAL RECORDS . . . . . . . . . . . . . . . . . 126

17. PARTY . . . . . . . . . . . . . . . . . . . . . . . . . 133

18. SHANNON AND J. J. . . . . . . . . . . . . . . . . . 139

19. PRESCRIPTIONS AND A VISITOR . . . . . . . . . . . 149

20. JUNIOR . . . . . . . . . . . . . . . . . . . . . . . . 159

21. PHILIP . . . . . . . . . . . . . . . . . . . . . . . . . 167

22. LORENA AND PHILIP . . . . . . . . . . . . . . . . . 174

23. DR. STRONG . . . . . . . . . . . . . . . . . . . . . 183

24. MATT . . . . . . . . . . . . . . . . . . . . . . . . . 190

25. SAYONARA . . . . . . . . . . . . . . . . . . . . . . 197

26. CAPTIVE . . . . . . . . . . . . . . . . . . . . . . . . . . . . . 203

27. QUESTIONS AND ANSWERS . . . . . . . . . . . . . . . . . . . . . 211

28. RESOLUTION . . . . . . . . . . . . . . . . . . . . . . . . . . . 221

ABOUT THE AUTHOR . . . . . . . . . . . . . . . . . . . . . . . . . 231

CHAPTER 1

# SHERIFF JOAN WILCOX

**B**urnet County Sheriff Joan Wilcox had become a family friend to both Mary Louise—my patient and understanding wife—and I after the Louis Devlin matter had been resolved. Devlin, originally from Kansas City and whose given name was Luigi Del Tommaso, had changed his name after a stint in prison in a failed attempt to "go straight" and leave his underworld roots behind. Unfortunately, as they say, your past catches up with you eventually, and how true that had been for Devlin. He had attempted to defraud a group of local investors involved in the construction of the new La Cava Golf Club and Estates. And, according to Del Andersen, owner of *The Highlander*, the local paper in Horseshoe Bay, Texas, his criminal partners were led by the notorious Nicky Savolio, Devlin's boyhood chum from the old Italian Kansas City neighborhood they both grew up in.

The feds and the media had invaded our little piece of Eden in the Texas Hill Country for months while the FBI and other government agencies tried to unravel Devlin's scheme to put at least $100 million in his and his criminal associates' pockets. Private sources said that Devlin took his chances and aligned himself with the Savolio family rather than turn state's evidence, thinking that a prison term was better than a death sentence from the Kansas City people. As it turned out, he got shanked while serving a fifteen-year term in Leavenworth for financial crimes, and he bled to death before the guards could come to his assistance.

While my day job consisted of performing the duties of an orthopedic surgeon specializing in hip and knee problems at the Hill Country Medical Center, I have repeatedly found myself embroiled in precarious situations in which I had no business. My foray into the Devlin business almost got me killed, and were it not for a herd of police officers and sheriff's deputies in the Hole in One Café having Sunday brunch, I would have gone to meet my Maker prematurely. Which would serve me right, some would probably say, as payback for Dr. James Robert Brady's recurrent involvement in matters of mystery and sometimes murder. Stick to your job, stick to what you know, stay out of trouble, people would say, including on occasion, Mary Louise, my long-suffering wife and partner of over thirty years. But she knew I had a penchant for trying to solve the unsolvable and she was supportive up to a point. When my life was put in danger, however, she drew the line, which is why I had been so good and unpredictably uncurious for the past year or more. But does a leopard change its spots? Hardly.

And so it was that I found myself seated in Sheriff Joan Wilcox's office, sipping a fresh cup of strong coffee that Sharon Baldwin, sheriff's deputy and factotum to the sheriff, had made. Deputy Baldwin specialized in massive designs for her hair, with multiple adornments. That day she had managed to weave her thick ropes through a pair of handcuffs which, despite how it sounded, was actually a statement in nouveau art.

Sharon was quite the contrast to her diminutive boss, who probably weighed no more than 110 pounds soaking wet, and whose pale complexion with freckles suggested an Irish heritage and a habit of minimal sun exposure. That morning, the sheriff had on a white dress shirt and a blazer, with her badge clipped onto the outside of the jacket pocket.

"You're dressed for a meeting?" I asked.

"Yes, oh great perceptive one. A meeting with the town council."

"Have you been bad again, Joan? Have you been showing up the boys in your investigations?"

"Nothing like that. They're worried about these last two murders, that we might have a serial killer in our midst."

There had been three murders in the past few months, all characterized by blows to the head with an instrument that resembled a hatchet, according to the coroner and chief of Hill Country Medical Center pathology, Dr. Jerry Reed.

"Do you have any clues?"

"Nothing, really. We've found three bodies, two female and one male, each behind a different convenience store in different areas of two counties, one in Burnet and two in Llano. The Llano County sheriff and I have spoken on several occasions and have included the chiefs of police of Marble Falls, Horseshoe Bay, Granite Falls, Granite Shoals, and Kingsland in the discussions, but to no avail. The only common factor in the three murders was a bag of groceries found at each crime scene, as though each victim was attacked after exiting the store."

"Each attack occurred in the evening, I assume?"

"Yes. Each was estimated to have occurred between 10 p.m. and one in the morning."

"That's pretty late for grocery shopping, don't you think, Joan?"

"Yes, but if you think about it, there are plenty of reasons to go out or be out late. We found nothing to relate the victims to each other in any way."

"So, why am I here, in danger of missing my tee time?"

I tried to reserve Friday afternoons and Saturday mornings for golf games with my bandit friends. Sometimes an emergency would arise on Thursday, and I would have to take care of it on Friday, but I had slowed my work schedule down a bit to try and preserve my quality time, also known as my mental health time.

"When Sharon called your office to schedule this meeting, she was told that you had to be on the road by 11 a.m. so as not to miss your tee time. It's 10:30, and we're almost done."

"Good. I appreciate that. The thing is, I don't know why you called me. I'm an orthopedic surgeon and try not to get in harm's way these days. I try and stick to my own business, stay out of trouble."

"That might be true, but you will never stay out of harm's way and mind your own business. I called Mary Louise yesterday and told her I was asking you to meet with me about these cases. I thought if you reviewed them, you might have a fresh perspective on the killings."

"This is a first for me, having a law enforcement representative contact me for assistance. Normally I would have to beg for scraps of information and plead for permission to get involved in such matters."

"I came to know Assistant Special Agent in Charge Susan Beeson well during the Devlin investigation, and she showed me how useful you could be in certain situations and investigations. And I felt I owed you a debt of gratitude for your support during my re-election campaign. And so here we are."

Susan Beeson was one of our oldest friends. She had been Houston's Chief of Police, following in her father's footsteps, when she accepted the position of ASAC of the FBI, Austin bureau. She and I had been paired through eight or nine crimes of different sorts over the years. She even had a badge made for me during a Houston investigation some years back. I kept it framed in my office. It was much safer there than in my possession. I had been shot at a few times, mugged, concussed, and run off the I-10 freeway in Houston. I could understand Mary Louise's concern for my safety. When I carried that badge, it, for me, was a license to steal. Without the badge, reality set in and I was a little more cautious about where I stepped, because going "bare" reminded me of my limitations.

In addition, Joan Wilcox had been elected somewhat recently as the first female sheriff of Burnet County. Her predecessor had been a real horse's ass, part of the "good old boy" network that had prevailed in Central Texas for many years. Mary Louise and I had held a few fundraisers in her honor, and getting the doctors and nurses at the massive Hill Country Medical Center behind her candidacy had turned the tide in her favor.

Joan opened one of her desk drawers and pulled out a sheaf of papers held together by a large clip. "Here you go, Jim Bob."

She handed me the stack of paperwork. I stood and shook her hand.

"Thanks for this," I said. "I'll get back to you if and when I find something."

She stood. "No, thank YOU. I hope to speak with you soon."

On the way out, I stopped by Deputy Baldwin's desk. "That is some 'do you have today. Who would have ever thought? Handcuffs and hair. Sheer genius."

"Oh, Dr. Brady, you're so nice about my hair. Most people don't get it."

"Everyone must have a passion, Sharon. Yours is unconventional, but an example of nouveau art, nonetheless. I'll see you when I see you, Deputy."

CHAPTER 2

# MARY LOUISE

The sheriff's office was in the north end of Marble Falls, so I had two routes I could take to get to the Horseshoe Bay Golf Club. The northern route would take me around the north side of Lake LBJ, named after our thirty-sixth president, through Kingsland, Granite Shoals, and Highland Haven. The southern route would direct me south on Highway 281, around Lake Marble Falls and onto FM 2147, then west to the golf club. I chose the southern route, not that it was a more beautiful drive than the northern route, but in deference to my stomach, which was growling with hunger. There was a delightful little food truck stationed on FM 2147 in Cottonwood Shores which served the best ground beef tacos around, and so the decision was made for me.

Maria's tacos were a delectable delight, but messy due to her spicy pico de gallo loaded with jalapeños and tomatoes. She had given me extra paper products, and I had tried to trap the juices inside a cocoon of foil and napkins, but to no avail. By the time I arrived at HBGC, there were more taco fixings on my shirt and shorts than in my stomach. Rather than jump out of the truck at the valet stand, I let the young man take my clubs and put them on a golf cart while I went and parked under a large oak tree and finished my lunch.

When I was finished, I opened a bottle of water and tried to clean myself up, but when you try to rub away taco stains off white golf shorts or shirts, well, you get . . . more taco mess. I locked up the Tahoe and tried to do a better job in the men's room, but the damage was done. In my favor was the fact it was a men's game, and having cash in the correct denominations to pay one's debts was more important than red and green stains on one's clothing. Nonetheless, I got the usual catcalls upon my arrival at the driving range, hearing greetings like "Hello, taco boy," "How's Jalapeño Man?" and similar well-intentioned insults.

I looked at the tee sheet and saw that we had sixteen players, meaning four foursomes. I was paired with Chucky, T. O., and Kirb. In our group there was no need for last names, or legitimate first names.

"Gimme twenty," said Kirb, retired physician, money handler, and keeper of the all-important scores for our group.

I handed over two tens. He looked at the bills like they were covered in a deadly virus.

"What is this red and green liquid on the bills, Brady? Tacos again for lunch?"

"You bet, Kirb. Best tacos around town, if you ask me."

"Nobody asked you, Brady, and it would be nice if you could bring clean money for a change. I must wash these off, thanks to you."

Kirb, a retired ophthalmologist who still had 20–20 vision and could see a ball land on the green from two hundred yards away, slumped away to the water station and tried to clean my lunch off the currency. I felt guilty for a moment, then came to my senses, went to the practice range, and warmed up.

The first group teed off a little before noon, and the three others in succession after that. We all finished in under four hours, sort of the gold standard in golf play time. I broke 80 just barely on the Ram Rock course, which was good for me, and walked away with more money than the ante had cost. We each had a beer or two, shared some laughs, and vowed to do it again Saturday morning.

Mary Louise and I lived in Granite Falls, one of the many small communities around the Texas Highland Lakes, which was a chain of six freshwater reservoirs formed by six dams on the lower Colorado River. The two largest lakes were Buchanan and Travis, which provided the water supply for the region. The four smaller lakes were Inks, LBJ, Marble Falls, and Austin. All six lakes provided tourism for the region in the form of golf, fishing, and boating. Our home was up in the hills above Lake LBJ, as far away from the summer insect infiltration as we could get. Ours was a small street with four houses, protected by an electronic gate. Each lot was pie-shaped, narrow in the front entry area, but very wide in the back area, which provided each house a spectacular view of Lake LBJ.

Mary Louise's car was absent from its spot in the garage, I noted, as I entered through the connecting garage door which emptied into a small mudroom adjacent to the kitchen. I heard no sounds from inside the house other than the excited barking of Tip, our aging golden retriever, who greeted me as if I had been gone for years.

"Hey, boy. Where's your mama?" I asked.

He tilted his head to the side, much like the old RCA dog, but didn't reveal her whereabouts. I patted his fat head, put him on the leash, and took him for a walk in the backyard. The rear of the property had a stunning lake view and was partially covered by a large wooden deck filled with comfortable chairs, tables, and various umbrellas and potted plants. I usually let Tip run free in the backyard, but several months back he had found a lovely pile of rabbit droppings and wallowed in the gummy mess to the extent Mary Louise had to take him to the vet's office for a cleanup on a Saturday. That had been my mistake, and I offered to cancel my golf game and take him myself, but she took it upon herself to take care of "my dog" and his problem. But then, she is just that type of girl.

I let the leash out as far as it would go as Tip explored the far limits of our one-acre plot of land. The prior owner had constructed a three-foot stucco fence around the rear of the property. I had never figured out what the fence was for. It didn't block our view of the lake, but neither could that height of fence keep in or out any animal that wanted to either exit from or trespass into our domain. It seemed to me a silly waste of funds, but since it was not OUR waste of funds, I didn't really care. I surmised the fence would keep a small dog in, but then a dog that small would be subject to airborne predators such as hawks and owls, which in and of itself presented another set of problems.

Once Tip finished his business, we returned to the kitchen. I popped the top off a beer and found a note in the bar fridge from Mary Louise. It read:

Gone to Austin for charity board meeting. Back around 6. Will bring dinner. Love, ML.

I took the opportunity to shower and shave, after which I constructed myself an eighteen-year Macallan single-malt scotch. Tip and I returned to comfortable seats on the terrace, and after a brief nap we heard the garage door open. He tore back inside like there was a house afire, and I followed.

"How are my boys?" said Mary Louise.

"Wow. You look stunning. Looks to me like you might have had a lunch date with another man. I mean, a red business suit, matching heels, and good David Webb jewelry. Who was the lucky guy?"

"Before I answer, please know there is no 'bad' David Webb jewelry. That said, what about a hug?"

She walked over to me and gave me an open-mouth kiss with not a small amount of passion in it. I pulled back and looked at her beautiful face. Her hair appeared to have been prepared professionally in a "down" position, partially curled and arranged in a layered cut of some sort.

"Let's see," she said, as she smelled my face. "You had two beers with the guys after golf, then came home and walked Tip while you had another. Then you showered and shaved, lathered yourself with that Stetson aftershave which you know I love, and built a scotch. Is that close?"

"You know me so well."

"Are you starving, or does this lady have time to clean up and change into something more . . . comfortable?"

"Yes, you do. I can put the food into the warmer oven. What is it, by the way?"

"Trader Joe's version of chicken parmesan and rigatoni pasta, with a Caesar salad to start."

"Okay. Salad to the big fridge, chicken parmesan and pasta to the warming oven, and I will bring you a cold glass of Rombauer chardonnay to the boudoir."

"A man after my own heart," she said, and sashayed into her bathroom.

I performed my duties and added a little scotch to my glass while I listened to the bathtub fill. After what I judged was the appropriate amount of time, I knocked politely, heard her say

"Entrez," and ventured into the wondrous bathroom space of Mary Louise Brady. The smells of cosmetics and perfumes permeated the air. I became dizzy with the sweet smells of my wife and, as always, wondered what she ever saw in me. We met when I was a poor medical student, while I was shopping for a birthday present for my mother. She was working behind the counter of an upscale store in Houston, doing some sort of externship from the business school at SMU in Dallas.

"Did you ever tell me why you were working in Houston instead of Dallas back when we met?" I said, handing her the wine.

"Yes. I explained that I had grown up in Dallas, went to SMU, and wanted to get away from my routine surroundings. One of my professors in marketing had come from Houston and thought I should become familiar with a totally different kind of shopping experience for my externship. I had an aunt who lived in Houston, so I intended to spend three or four months there and then return to Dallas. But you had other things in mind, did you not, kind sir?"

"You betcha."

It was difficult to look at her face, considering her ample chest was floating right there in front of me in her bathtub.

"What are you thinking right now?"

"That I would like to strip down and get in there with you."

"And do you need a formal invitation?"

"I don't know. Do I?"

"Hardly."

One thing led to another, and shortly we were frolicking in the warm tub together.

After a time, when we were spent and our drinks finished, we dried each other off, dressed in terry-cloth robes, and headed to the kitchen to prepare dinner. I tossed the salad while Mary Louise heated up and seasoned the chicken parmesan and rigatoni pasta. I poured us each a glass of Rombauer chardonnay, and we sat at the kitchen bar and ate.

"What's the stack of papers in the clip?" she asked.

"Documents our newly re-elected sheriff gave me this morning."

"Joan Wilcox? Ah yes, Joan called me about this. I didn't want to tell you until it happened. What did she say to you?"

"Well, she had asked me to drop by, which I did. She thanked me—both of us, actually—for helping her get elected again. And to ask my assistance in a case."

Mary Louise stopped chewing and stared at me for a moment before breaking into a small smile. "So, for—what, twenty years or so?—you've involved yourself in all sorts of murder and mystery cases and have had to literally beg law enforcement to let you assist because of some crazy idea you had, which most often turned out to be correct, I might add. And now, after all this time, our sheriff has come to you and asked you to help. How are you feeling about that?"

"Well, I was surprised. She probably told you it's about the three murder victims who had head trauma caused by an instrument that may resemble an axe or hatchet of some sort."

"My least-favorite part of the story."

"Joan gave me this stack of papers and asked me to review the cases, see if I had any ideas. She said the town council, or county council, or whatever they call the people that run Burnet County, have her under the gun, so to speak. The county coffers are feeling the decline in tourism that comes with a possible serial killer. Joan has few clues, so she thought, what could it hurt for me to take a look?"

"My conversation with Joan was fairly brief, but we both agreed it was probably safer for you if you were brought in at this point, doing something you could do at home, rather than having you once again dive in with your own personal on-site investigation. And I'm pleased that she recognizes how valuable your insights can be. Did she mention whether she'd be working with Susan Beeson? They worked together during the Devlin business, right?"

"Yes. And I mentioned Susan to Joan when we met. I imagine that would be the next logical step, that she'll call Susan and ask for governmental assistance."

"Since Joan is newly re-elected, I could see how she might want to solve this without bringing in the feds, since they usually take over the case, right?"

"Yes."

"Maybe she needs to prove herself even further than being elected sheriff, as women often need to do."

"Men have to prove themselves as well."

"Remind me how many years you boys had the right to vote and we women did not?"

"I forget, Mary Louise. Quite a while."

"Quite a while is the correct answer. You just watch yourself, young man—in general, but also working on this case. You would not be nearly as attractive with an axe buried in the side of *your head.*"

"You know that I will, as always, be careful, and try not to put myself in any untoward danger."

"I've heard that storyline before, Jim Bob Brady, and when you get involved in one of these mysteries, you seem to throw caution to the wind. Just please be careful. And don't tell me 'yes dear.' You know I hate that."

"I will do my best to maintain an attitude of caution. Remember, I'm just reading some reports. I am not going out into the field to do battle."

"In my experience, that is just a matter of time."

CHAPTER 3

# THE VICTIMS

I volunteered to clean up our dinner mess and take Tip for his final walk of the day. Mary Louise's eyes were closing as we completed our meal, so I reasoned that she had the worst day between us, what with having to drive over to Austin and back. She bussed my cheek, mumbled a sleepy I love you, and went to bed. Tip whined, that being his signal to please take him out so he could do his business and then run back to cuddle up to Mary Louise in bed. I obliged him and made note that he did his business ever-so-quickly and scurried back into the house for his alone time with the matron of the house.

My Saturday tee time was not until 11 a.m., so I refreshed my Macallan and took the paperwork from Joan Wilcox to my favorite recliner in the great room and started to read.

The first victim was Hubert Brown, a fifty-six-year-old radiologic technician at Hill Country Medical Center. He was found three months ago outside a combination small grocery and gas station two miles from the hospital. The camera from the pump area showed that he arrived at 9:48 p.m., filled the tank on his three-year-old Ford Bronco, then went inside to purchase items to take with him to work. The indoor camera over the checkout area filmed his purchase of an energy cola, Cheetos, peanut butter crackers, and a pack of Marlboro Lights. The attendant called him by name, confirming the information supplied to law enforcement by the cashier that Brown often stopped at that location on his way to the hospital and that he was known by the staff.

It was about 10:05 p.m. when the attendant, name of Charles Atwood, noticed that Brown's Bronco was still in the pump station area. The store was empty at that time, so he left his post and ran out to the SUV to check on Mr. Brown. He was not in the car or under the car. Atwood, upon his return trek toward the store, heard a noise coming from the rear of the building. He had experience with burglaries, especially late in the evening, so he went into the bodega, went behind the counter, grabbed his Colt .45 caliber revolver for which he had a license, and went out the hidden door in the back of the store to explore the rear of the property. He immediately saw Mr. Brown lying on the concrete with a massive head wound and an extreme amount of blood pouring from his skull. He was near the trash cans and was attempting to bang his foot against the metal cans, either to attract attention and hopefully be rescued, or as the result of some sort of reflex mechanism due to the head injury.

Atwood leaned down, careful not to touch Mr. Brown or his surroundings. Brown mumbled some words which Atwood could not understand. Atwood immediately called 911 and related his findings. He had been a medic in the Marine Corps and knew impending death when he saw it. He later told the investigating officers that Mr. Brown was in the throes of death when Atwood found the victim, and the situation was hopeless. He did not attempt resuscitation efforts, and he avoided touching the body because he assumed it was a murder and didn't want to disturb the crime scene.

Video cameras inside and outside the property corroborated Atwood's story. The actual murder had been outside the view of the rear video camera, as it was blank except for showing the victim's foot next to the garbage cans. Brown was dead by the time 911 responders arrived. The coroner's technicians pronounced him dead on the scene, and cause of death was said to be massive blood loss from a severe open head injury. He was autopsied the next day at HCMC by Dr. Jerry Reed, chief of pathology and coroner for Burnet County. The autopsy revealed no medical problems except for early emphysema due to smoking. The head wound literally split the suture lines in the cranium, and the blow from the object took out part of the victim's left ear and most of his parietal lobe, and went through the cranial vault into and past the pituitary gland, severing the middle cerebral artery. Death should have been instantaneous, Reed opined, but unfortunately for Mr. Brown it was not. The wound was created with superhuman force, he wrote in the autopsy report, by an object resembling a hatchet or small axe with an extremely sharp edge. He took tissue samples to evaluate for DNA material, should the need arise for possible future matching procedures.

Detectives from Burnet County had delved into Mr. Brown's past, his family, and his work environment, looking for clues. Brown had been divorced for many years, and his ex-wife had not spoken to him in a couple of months. He had three grown children and four grandchildren, and according to interviews with the family members, he was not close to any of his immediate family.

Detectives spoke to Brown's supervisor and his coworkers at HCMC and found that Brown liked the night shift, that he was not a "people person" and preferred the quiet of working in the middle of the night. He did an adequate job, nothing stellar to report, but then no tell-tale clues about his slaying were discovered, either.

Burnet County had a fund that offered a reward for information relating to unsolved murders, through a dedicated hotline. There had been, as usual, a few crank calls, but nothing substantive had been found. The case was at a dead end.

The second murder occurred about a month after the first. That victim was a forty-five-year-old female by the name of Delores White who was slain in a similar manner as Hubert Brown. Burnet County detectives pieced together that she had completed her shift as a short-order cook at a local all-night dive at approximately 11 p.m. She had stopped on her way home at a Stop and Go on Highway 281. All the bays with gas pumps were full, so she had parked on the side of the building, which was unlit. She entered the store, bought eggs, butter, milk, and a few canned goods. The attendant had seen her before, but not well enough to know her name. The victim had purple hair, which was why the attendant remembered her.

Ms. White's body was found when the attendant who had remembered the purple hair went out a back door to smoke a cigarette and discovered her body tangled up with the refuse cans in the rear. He ran back inside the store and called 911 and told his coworker what had happened. They both kept weapons under the counter, produced them, locked the front door, turned the Closed sign on, then went back and hid behind the counter in case the killer was still on premises.

The coroner's investigators team pronounced the victim dead at the scene. Dr. Jerry Reed again performed the autopsy, which produced similar findings as the first. Ms. White had a skull that was thinner and smaller than Mr. Brown's, so even though the wound entered the left side of the skull, it was of such force that the murder weapon went all the way through the skull and dented the interior of the opposite, or right, side. Dr. Reed wrote in his report that he might consider the assailant was right-handed due to the blow originating on the left side of the skull, but he could not swear to it. There was no evidence of foreign material in the vicinity of the wound, but he took tissue samples to match future DNA material, should it be found.

Ms. White had little family to speak of. Her mother lived with her and had dementia, and she basically knew nothing about her daughter, or any other family member, for that matter. Ms. White had been married a long time ago but had been divorced for years and had no children. As far as a suspect or a reason for her murder, it was another dead end.

The last murder had occurred a month prior and was the saddest of the three. Not that all murders are not sad, but the last one involved a teenager. Bart Smalls and his girlfriend had stopped at the HEB in Marble Falls at midnight for beer and snacks. They were both seniors in high school, were eighteen years old, and had good fake IDs. He had been out partying, it being Friday night. The girlfriend, Noni Berry, had been babysitting, and Bart had picked her up from her job and wanted to drink some more beer and go make out. The parking lot was full for that time of night, so Bart had parked farther away from the entry than he wanted. Noni was tired, so she waited in the car while he went into the HEB. Cameras showed Bart with a grocery basket inside the store, where he dumped a case of beer into the bottom of the basket and covered it with all varieties of snacks—crackers, chips, jerky, and the like. He was in the store for twenty minutes and managed to get through with all his purchases, including the beer, even though the staff was diligent in looking for fake IDs.

When he reached the car, he didn't see Noni in the passenger seat. He walked around the driver's side of the car and on to the trunk, intending to put in his purchases, and he found her there.

He started screaming and was heard by a passerby, who called 911. Police officers were in the area and responded quickly. No one knew what to do with the body folded into the trunk, covered in blood. The first responders had powerful flashlights that clearly showed the brain wound, again on the left side. When the coroner's techs arrived, they did their best to avoid contaminating the crime scene, which was difficult, due to the process of getting the body out of the trunk.

Detectives were called, and they reviewed the feed from the video cameras from all angles along the storefront as well as the parking lot. Bart's car was seen from a distance, but only the front fender and license plate were visible. The detectives pondered about the luck or skill of the assailant in avoiding camera detection. They had also investigated the prior two homicides and were well-versed in the crime-scene patterns of all three cases.

Dr. Jerry Reed performed the autopsy the following day and noted the same findings as the two prior cases. The wound in Noni's head started on the left side, as it did in the two prior homicides. Again Dr. Reed harvested tissue samples for potential DNA sampling. Noni had no significant findings on autopsy other than the head wound.

Both sets of parents were interviewed the following day. Noni's parents were beside themselves, railing about how Bart was no good and a bad influence on their daughter. She had never been in trouble and was an A student and a member of the National Honor Society. Without Bart's influence she would be alive, sleeping late, and enjoying her weekend off. It was all Bart's fault, they opined. Their family was composed of good people, church-going people, who obeyed the law. Noni had unfortunately become tied up with Bart, who came from a questionable background and had been in jail.

Bart's parents were another story. Reading between the lines, the detectives thought the apple didn't fall far from the tree. Both parents were on probation, having served time for drug use and distribution. The house reeked of cigarette smoke, with beer bottles and empty whiskey bottles strewn everywhere; the house was a nasty mess. The parents were in their late thirties, having become parents when they were not that much older than their son. Bart was not home, and they had no idea where he was. Despite their legal troubles and a lousy living environment, nothing came from the interview to indicate that there was a palpable reason coming from the household that resulted in the murder of Noni Berry. After a few more weeks of pointless investigation, the case was at a standstill.

By then, it was after midnight, and I was whipped. I slipped into bed as quietly as I could so as not to disturb my sleeping wife nor my guardian dog. Dreams of heads being chopped off came and went during my sleep, and I wondered if reading about dismal murder scenes was the best way to spend my free time.

# CHAPTER 4

# THE RUNNER

"**W**hat's on your agenda today?" I asked a sleepy Mary Louise as we drank coffee on the terrace. It was a beautiful fall morning, with a slight coolness to the air indicative of the winter that was to come. Tip had already eaten his breakfast and done his business and was now sleeping at our feet, recovering from his rigorous morning activities.

"I have some errands to run, plus it's beauty day—hair and nails. Are you golfing?"

"Yep, it being Saturday and all."

"Did you stay up and read about the murder cases? From the looks of those little bags under your eyes, I would say yes."

"I did. Not the sort of fare one should read about before trying to sleep. Pretty gruesome stuff."

"Did you have any breakthroughs on the cases? How many are there?"

"Three murders thus far."

"Does that mean there will be more?"

"No idea, but since Joan asked me to review the files, she must be desperate. This is fall, which usually consists of great weather months, not to mention it's football season. Let me think, golf, fishing, boating, and football, all in the same day. Who wouldn't want to be on a lake in the Hill Country? Oh, but wait, there's a serial killer lurking about the local grocery stores, anxious to bury a hatchet in your head. We'd better stay home until the killer has been caught, thinks the potential traveling family unit. And that's the motivation of the county leadership, who have imparted that same motivation to the sheriff and her minions. Tourism means money, and money makes the world go round."

"That's a rather jaded view, husband. What about the people who've been killed? What about preservation of lives?"

"That's another point of view, Mary Louise. And I didn't say that the so-called jaded view was MY view. It's the view of the powers that be, which entrusted me with these documents to enlist my assistance in finding this nasty miscreant who, in my opinion, must have some horrible mental illness. Think about it. He—it's most likely a 'he'—lurks about grocery store parking lots late at night, bludgeons his victims with a sharp hatchet or axe, and does not—wait a minute. Did he take anything from the victims? I don't remember," I said, and returned inside, retrieved the documents, and started looking back through the files.

"*Could* the assailant be a female?"

"Possible, but she would have to be strong to wield the killing object and do that much damage to the skull. My guess is a male, strong, and criminally insane. Though I'm no expert on that."

"I can say that these murders certainly represent a level of violence that seems like it would be, at the very least, a case of temporary insanity, if you will."

She watched me for a moment before asking, "What are you looking for?"

"I'm looking for missing items from the victims, some object that they each would be expected to possess. Like a wallet, or keys, something each would need upon entering a store to purchase items. There's no mention by the detectives of anything missing from the victims. I just wonder . . ."

"Call Joan. She's probably in the office on a Saturday morning."

I did just that. Sharon Baldwin answered the sheriff's private phone line. "Dr. Brady, how nice to hear from you. How may I help you this fine morning?"

"Any chance of speaking to your boss?"

"She's in a meeting but will be done in half an hour. May I have her call you?"

"That would be great, Sharon. Thanks much."

Sheriff Joan Wilcox returned my call after an hour or so. I took that time to get dressed for my golf game at noon. "What can I do for you, Jim? Have you looked through the reports?"

"I have, and I can't find notations of anything missing from any of the victims. Do you have any other information that might reveal that?"

"Huh. Let me ask the two Ds that are investigating the case. They're both here in my office."

I heard some murmuring and muttering through the phone, then a male raised voice, probably objecting to my presence in their cases.

"I'm just now finding this out, but there was an odd object missing from each victim. The two males were each carrying a wallet in their left rear pocket. There were credit cards present, as well as cash. But each was missing his driver's license. In the case of the female victim, she had a purse nearby containing a wallet with cash and credit cards, as well as car keys. But nothing was missing except her driver's license. I cannot believe I'm just hearing this for the first time."

"Would that not be an odd thing to steal, the driver's license off a person you had just killed, and leave cash and credit cards intact?"

"I think so. In fact, that would tend to imply that the murderer needed some sort of identification to prove he had killed the right person. That would tend to contradict our opinion that the three murders were totally random. I wonder what else my detectives might have overlooked, thinking it was not important information in solving these cases. We'll have our discussion about that after I hang up. Anything else you can think of, Jim?"

"No, not at this time. I didn't intend to get your detectives in trouble, Joan."

"They should have appreciated that evidence themselves and brought it to me. I thank you for your diligence. We'll speak later," she said, and hung up.

"One day on the job and already it sounds like you've alienated the professionals. Good luck in getting any help from the detectives."

"Mary Louise, I was just following up on an observation. I certainly didn't mean to get them in trouble."

"Jim Bob, after all these years, I have learned that you stumble onto more undiscovered information than any other human being I have ever known. You have a gift. That is why Joan wanted you to review the files, to get a fresh perspective on the murders. You cannot help it that you happen to rub people the wrong way in making new discoveries. That is the Jim Bob way!"

I made it to the golf course on time and went through the motions of playing golf. I was distracted by the notion of the murderer collecting driver's licenses of his victims. What in the world was that about? I was so distracted that I missed a four-foot putt on the eighteenth hole, which put my team out of the money for the day. I left after the golf game was done; having endured enough boos and catcalls over the missed putt, I avoided further abuse after the round by declining my usual beer or two.

On the drive home, I pondered the logic of a seemingly mentally troubled person taking the time after bludgeoning someone to death to retrieve a form of identification. What could that mean? What was the point? Were we dealing with a hired killer who was required to provide formal identification of his victims to an employer? Or was collecting ID a fetish of some sort, to be reviewed by the killer in quiet times between murders?

Then I wondered if maybe there was some sort of connection between the victims that was not apparent. Maybe I had missed something in my review of the files. I decided I should review the paperwork again, go over the documents with a fine-toothed comb, and see if I had missed something. I was concentrating so hard on the possible interconnections that I missed my turn into our street. I told myself I missed it because fall was upon us, and daylight was starting to wane early, even though it was only a little past 5 p.m. There was a dog park at the bottom of the hill, so rather than make a U-turn, I decided to drive around the park and return to our street entrance. There were a few folks walking their beloved pets, and a couple even had flashlights out already.

Out of the corner of my eye I saw a flash off to my right. It looked like a figure was running, and at first glance I thought it was a dog that had gotten loose from their leash. Then the figure morphed into a small person running, and I wondered why they would be running across the diagonal of the park rather than around the groomed track. Then I glimpsed a glint of shiny metal in the runner's right hand, and in my mind's eye I envisioned the hatchet killer. I started honking the horn, saw his—at least it appeared to be a male figure— head turn my way, but he kept on running. I continued to drive around the park but had to stop at each right angle to avoid injury to canines or pedestrians.

By the time I reached the opposite side, the runner was gone. I stupidly opened the door, jumped out, and followed the trail of the runner, but he was nowhere to be seen. The park sat on a small mesa, and on the outskirts of the park were hills descending in all directions, loaded with mesquite and oak trees, with plenty of places to hide in the waning daylight. I came to my senses and returned to the truck, got in and locked the door, and decided to make another pass around the dog park before turning onto my street.

No one still walking appeared distressed, so perhaps I was the only person who saw the runner with what I presumed was his weapon. I stopped a couple of folks and asked if they had seen what I had seen, and both looked at me as though I were unstable. I made the block, turned onto our home street, went up the hill, and opened the electronic gate with a transponder. I kept a keen eye on the rearview mirror and the side mirrors but saw no one. I opened the garage door with the remote, pulled in, and remained in the locked truck until the door closed behind me. I realized when I opened the garage door that empties into the mudroom that I was shaking uncontrollably.

CHAPTER 5

# MONDAY, MONDAY

**S**unday was normally a couples' golf day for Mary Louise and me. She had taken up the game later in life and, unlike yours truly, was content to hit the golf ball down the middle, get on the green, and make putts. My goal was to hit the ball as far as possible, then go looking through the weeds and water for it. With a handicap of twenty-two, she was almost unbeatable. I was proud of my handicap of ten although several "gimme putts" were usually necessary for me to maintain golf scores at that level. I was probably a fifteen or sixteen handicapper, but that just did not sound good to a man with my FORMER skills.

We played the Slick Rock course at Horseshoe Bay Golf Club that Sunday with another couple by the name of Bob and Annie Jackson. She was Mary Louise's since-childhood best friend, and a scratch golfer. She was petite, small in every aspect, but could muster a swing of 100 mph and knock the cover off the ball. Bob was a car dealer, and everything in his life was exaggerated. He had what we fondly call a beer belly, and was loud, drank too much, and talked much more than he needed to. But he was hysterically funny, constantly telling jokes, and thus was a great golf partner, and every outing with him ended in a stellar day.

It was a club tournament day, and the format was better ball of the women plus better ball of the men. Each of us were on our game that day, and we won the event, defeating the twenty-two other teams handily. Afterward, there was a large seating area indoors that had room for most of the players, but we opted to sit outside, the day being beautiful with a cloudless blue sky and temperature in the mid-70s.

"Have you heard about this murderer on the loose, killing people with an axe or something?" Bob asked.

We were eating hamburgers cooked medium rare—in other words, juicy—and discussing the killer and his victims probably was not the best dinner conversation.

"I have, Bob, but maybe now is not the best time to talk about it," I said.

"Really, Bobby, give it a rest. I don't want to think about that while I eat," Annie said.

"I hear tell there have been three of them now, different kinds of people, in different locations. You're tight with the new sheriff of Burnet County, so I figured maybe she gave you the inside scoop," said Bob.

"No," I lied. "I know only what I've read in the papers."

"Huh. You're supposed to be some sort of amateur detective, so I thought maybe you might be assisting our marginally competent law enforcement."

"No, Bob, I'm just doing my doctor day job and trying to keep a low profile and stay out of trouble. And besides, my more recent experience with the local law enforcement has been excellent, so I consider them capable of handling the investigation into the murders."

Mary Louise was fortunately quiet on the matter. I had told her of my experience the day before with the runner I saw in the park, and although I didn't know what to make of it, the fact that there was a runner in our neighborhood possibly brandishing a weapon was disconcerting. I was glad she was silent. I did not want to discuss the issue further because Bob would tell everyone he knew everything he heard, and I felt the need to keep the facts to myself, at least in deference to Sheriff Wilcox.

"Another beer, Brady? It's on me."

"In that case, yes."

While Bob was at the bar procuring drinks, Annie expressed aloud her concern for her husband. "Do you think he drinks too much, Jim Bob?"

"We all probably drink too much, Annie."

"But Bob has become a daytime drinker. In the past, he would start drinking after 5 p.m., but now, he sometimes starts at noon. And you know how he gets."

"Yes, I do. Is there something going on with him? The business, maybe?"

"Business is fine, never better, in fact, according to Bob. I was hoping you would talk to him."

"Annie, I try to stay out of my friends' businesses. That is how you keep your friends. You tolerate their shortcomings."

"But I'm worried. He's been passing out at dinner from drinking all day. I talked to his doctor about it, but he's afraid to say anything. Please?"

I looked at Mary Louise. She smiled and patted my hand.

"I'll think about it, Annie. Just not today. Let him enjoy our victory."

Bob returned with drinks. We toasted each other and celebrated the win.

On the way home, Mary Louise was unusually quiet.

"Are you okay?"

"Yes, just thinking about things. Annie is so worried about Bob's drinking. I don't know what to say or do anymore."

"I haven't noticed him being particularly different. He seems to be the same old Bob to me. What am I missing?"

"He is mostly the same old Bob around friends. It's that when they're alone, or he's alone, he starts drinking and continues until he's nearly comatose. He passes out at night, and Annie is afraid he may stop breathing."

"Good grief. I've never seen him like that."

"According to her, it happens all the time. And as if that's not enough to worry about, we may have a serial killer in our midst."

"I shared my experience from yesterday with you not with the intent to frighten you, just to make you aware of circumstances that might eventually involve us in some way or another. After previous events involving the Savolio family and the Devlin family and the Fixer, we both have carry permits, and we both can shoot, especially you. You're deadly with that Glock 19, so I think you can fend for yourself if the need were to arise."

"And I thank you for all your efforts in that regard. I feel much safer knowing how to defend myself."

"As well you should. I feel sorry for any miscreant that crosses your path. What was it the instructor called you?"

She laughed. "Bloody Mary. Because of all the targets I shot the bulls eye out of, and the silhouette kills on the competition course."

"That's right. Bloody Mary. Too funny."

We arrived home to a somewhat desperate dog. We walked outside with him and sat on the terrace for a bit. "I would ask you if you wanted a drink, but after hearing the story about Bob, maybe water is in order?"

"Water sounds perfect, Jim Bob."

I opened us each a bottle of Fiji water, and we sat in the cool of the evening and enjoyed the stars and each other's company.

Monday morning brought reality to bear. I worked as an orthopedic surgeon specializing in hip and knee replacement at Hill Country Medical Center, a thriving medical institution that was technically in Marble Falls, Texas, but serviced a population of close to 100,000 in Burnet, Llano, and the surrounding counties. At one time, the closet tertiary treatment facility was in Austin, but a core of investors led by Dr. Buck Owens, a former family doctor, put together the HCMC with the idea that folks in our neck of the woods deserved first-class medical care without having to make the trek to Austin, Houston, or Dallas. HCMC had the capability of treating all but the worst of injuries and medical problems, which were known as the Level I problems. It maintained its status as a Level II facility, and even had a heliport for inbound and outbound patients.

HCMC had doctors from every specialty represented, with facilities to care for cardiac and neurosurgical problems. There were two large structures present on the campus: the hospital building, which housed the beds for patients, MRI and CT scanning facilities, and a physical therapy unit, and the clinic building, with doctor's offices, patient examination areas, and outpatient x-ray. The hospital side also housed a certified rehabilitation unit for aftercare that might be needed following operations such as hip and knee replacement. Each structure had three stories, and each story of the hospital was connected to its mate on the clinic side via enclosed walkways. This prevented the elements of weather from interfering in the ebb and flow of patient care.

Over the years, HCMC had gradually aligned itself with other medical institutions, forming a coalition of health care providers that boasted over 5,000 physicians and 35,000 employees. Hill Country Medical Center was a first-class facility, and I was proud to be part of the medical staff. I had spent many years in Houston working at the University Medical Center, and I could honestly say that the facilities at HCMC were just as fine as those in Houston but without the traffic snarls.

I met Belinda Brooks, a certified nurse practitioner and my trusted and invaluable surgical assistant, at 6 a.m. in our offices on the third floor of the HCMC clinic building. Belinda had been working with me for a while now, and she had become a most reliable second pair of hands, working in the operating room. She was a large-boned woman and strong, which was essential in the business of hip and knee replacement surgery. Belinda had gone to Texas A&M on an athletic scholarship in wrestling, and originally her plan was to eventually compete in the Olympics. However, as life often does—we plan, God laughs—she was thrown a curve with a knee injury during the SEC wrestling championship. After the ACL and ligamentous repair, she was pronounced well for most activities . . . except wrestling, her passion and joy. Her contact with multiple orthopedic surgeons, however, piqued her interest in medicine. The family finances were not in good shape after she lost her college scholarship, so rather than pursue an expensive and lengthy training program in medicine, she opted for nursing school and a nurse practitioner career. She had grown up in nearby Johnson City and found her way to HCMC for nurse practitioner training. Her loss was perhaps not a loss, however, because Belinda loved what we did for a living and even loved being on call on the weekends, handling emergencies for the physician staff.

"Morning, Doc. How was your weekend?"

"Long and luscious, thanks to you. Was it a bad weekend for you?"

"I was on call for the emergency room, and it was active. Nothing for you, however. There were several injured young people from the Llano Livestock Show and Rodeo, but the hip and knee injuries were minimal. Mostly hands and shoulders and elbows this weekend."

"Lucky for me. Well, what's our lineup today?"

"We have six cases: three hip replacements, two knee replacements, and an ankle replacement. No redo hips, which I sort of miss, but which you do not."

The hardest part of my job was revision hip replacements. Many had been cemented in position, and getting all that cement out of the pelvis, acetabulum, and femur was a bear. I had decided to decline to do revision hips, except for revisions to those hips I myself had previously worked on, of course. This had freed up my schedule quite a bit, such that I was able to get patients in for surgery quicker, and my operating days were less stressful and less physically demanding.

"Any leftovers in the hospital?"

"No, sir. The last two from last Wednesday's schedule were moved over to the rehab unit yesterday. No rounds to make except in rehab, which we can do after surgery if you like."

"That sounds good. I'll catch up here in the office, get a bite to eat, and meet you in the OR."

"Yes, sir."

I signed off on a few charts, re-dictated operative reports that the medical records department insisted I had missed, and opened the mail. Fortunately, there were no envelopes with green tape indicating certified mail, the hallmark of lawsuit letters from plaintiff's attorneys, which struck fear in the hearts of all surgeons. I had been around the block long enough to accept the realities of medical litigation, but then I had not been sued in years, and my personal animus about it had receded. There was a time, many years ago, when I had been involved in such a lawsuit, having been wrongly accused of causing a patient to lose an extremity after a total knee replacement. I was eventually vindicated, but not without the price of a concussion and a hospital stay. But then, that was another story.

I greeted a few colleagues in the doctors' dining area outside the operating room and had a "light" breakfast of bacon, eggs, and hash browns. After all, one did need one's strength to do the kind of work I did. Cholesterol be damned, I say.

Belinda and I said good morning to the patients who were checked in, greeted the families, and took a black marker and drew an incisional line along the extremity to be repaired. I had never operated on the wrong extremity, but I had been involved in such a case back in my training program in which the private attending surgeon was struggling with a knee ligament repair and called for a resident assistant. I happened to be available, and after scrubbing in, I looked at the X-rays hung on the light screens, which was my routine, and noticed all the pictures were of the RIGHT knee. The attending surgeon was attempting to cut a notch in the femur bone in the LEFT knee. I made the comment that he was operating on the wrong extremity, and that I would be leaving him to his own fate.

He tried to get me fired for leaving him in the lurch, something like dereliction of duty, but eventually nothing ever came of it. The doctor was a hack and lost his operating privileges, but he moved on to another institution soon thereafter and was back in business before long. It was not easy to police doctors, especially surgeons, and even harder to get a bad actor's license revoked.

We started in the first room at 7 a.m. with a hip replacement. Once the bone work was done and the prostheses inserted, Belinda went about closure of the muscle and skin and dressing application while I began the hip replacement next door. We continued with that routine, going back and forth between the two rooms until all six cases were done, which was a little after 4 p.m. We spoke to all the families, then changed out of our surgical scrubs and into clean ones and made rounds on the patients who had made it to their respective rooms. We also stopped in at the rehab unit to check on those joint replacements from the prior week who had been transferred. We then went back to the recovery room and checked on the last two who had just awakened.

We returned to the office by 5 p.m. My administrative assistant, Maya Stern, had a few questions about scheduling, but other than that it was quiet for a Monday. Maya had been in my employ for a couple of years. She was the opposite of Belinda: short and petite, with dark features and jet-black hair. She had the good fortune—well, misfortune, actually—of coming into a good deal of money, as well as inheriting a home, when her aunt had been murdered the previous year, a mess I was involved in on the investigative side. She was smart, and so good with patients. I was a lucky man to have those two women working with me. Once I completed my paperwork duties, I left the building and headed home.

# CHAPTER 6

# BOB JACKSON

"How was your day?" asked Mary Louise as I entered my place of solace and support.

"Good," I said, as she handed me a newly constructed Macallan scotch. "And getting better," I said, as I sipped the finely aged eighteen-year-old whiskey and sat at the kitchen bar. "Are we eating in?"

"Yes. I try to prepare meals at home on surgery days so you can get some rest. Haven't you noticed that over the last, what, twenty or thirty years?" she said, smiling.

"Of course, and I appreciate your efforts, as always." She was barefoot and had on her favorite tee shirt that said I Love My Attitude Problem. It was my favorite too, because she had owned it a long time, and it was threadbare from all the washings and dryings, and therefore almost sheer.

"I should probably let you relax for a moment before disturbing your reverie with bad news, but Annie called earlier this afternoon and said Bob went on a bender at lunch and has not stopped drinking. That's about five hours of continuous alcohol consumption. How can someone tolerate that?"

"A lot of practice. Is there something you're wanting me to do?"

"Well, Annie said he's three sheets to the wind, so talking to him now would probably not do any good."

"What does she expect me to do?"

"I don't know, Jim Bob. Talk to him, get him some help?"

"You realize that you and Annie are much closer than Bob and I are."

"Yes, but she trusts you to handle things, and she's trying to keep information about this drinking issue limited to a small number of people."

"I don't have to do anything this evening, then?"

"No. Dinner will be ready in half an hour, so go shower and change and get comfortable. I just fed and walked Tip, so he's fine for now."

That would explain our dog's lethargy. He had barely acknowledged my arrival, which was unusual.

"Will do."

I took a long hot shower, letting my sore muscles feel the heat and relax after moving heavy anesthetized legs around all day. I did six cases each on Monday and Wednesday and saw clinic patients all day Tuesday and Thursday. Four days of work per week, with no redo hip replacements except the occasional one that I had done over the past twenty years or so. And I was still beat. I thought maybe I needed some vitamins. I was still strong and had endurance, but truth be known, I was not as young as I once was. My thoughts turned to Mary Louise, standing in the kitchen with that revealing tee shirt on. But unlike in my younger days, the wanton desire quickly evaporated and was replaced with hunger pangs.

"Want another drink?" she called, as I exited my bathroom.

"Maybe a glass of wine," I replied as I returned to the kitchen bar. "What are we having for dinner?"

"Meat loaf, mashed potatoes, string beans, and a salad to start."

"Chardonnay sounds good to me. How about you?"

"Perfect."

I opened a bottle of Newton unfiltered and poured each of us a glass into a nice goblet of Waterford crystal. We toasted, and I took the glasses to one of the tables on the terrace while Mary Louise set out the food in the kitchen. We helped ourselves buffet style and enjoyed a nice meal together as the light faded into oblivion.

"I hate getting older."

"Why do you say that? Men just get better with age."

"Well, I got . . . amorous, shall we say, in the shower. There was a time when wild horses could not drag me away from you when I was in that state. But the desire went away just as quickly as it arrived and was replaced by the feelings of hunger, of all things."

She laughed. "When dinner is done, and if you're still feeling in a family way, we can fix that problem quite easily. We have a great sex life, and you're the perfect partner."

"Well, nice of you to say, but I'm afraid the moment may have passed."

"Whatever you need, whenever you need it, I'm here for you. Don't ever forget that." She stood up, leaned over and gave me a big wet open-mouthed kiss. "Stay here and finish your wine and I'll clean up."

"I'd be happy to help," I said, but she pushed me back into the chair. "Sit. Enjoy yourself. You had a long day. I'll be back when I'm done."

Next thing I remembered was Mary Louise's arm around me, escorting me into the bed. I had fallen asleep outside.

"I walked Tip, and everything is fine. Get some sleep," she said, and tucked me in.

Belinda and I met on the third floor of the hospital side of HCMC at 6 a.m. Tuesday morning for rounds. The six post-op patients from the day before were all doing well, some using their respective morphine pumps more than others. Everyone was expected to get up the first day after surgery and sit in a bedside chair, then try and make the trek to the bathroom with the physical therapist. Hardly any patient ever thought they could make it that distance the day after a joint replacement, but they all eventually did. It was good for the mind to make the trip, giving the patient the sense that they would achieve independence eventually, and that all the pain and rehab would someday be worth it.

I picked up a breakfast sandwich in the doctor's lounge and made it to the clinic side to see patients starting at 7:05 a.m. I used four exam rooms, and all were full already. The schedule was quite busy, as Tuesday was usually busier than Thursday because of problems that developed over the weekend. Some patients were "callers" and were worried about each small detail of their recovery, making a lot of calls to the staff, even on the weekends. Other patients were the "stoics," who waited to see the doctor, hoping the problems would pass in time because they didn't want to bother the staff or consider there might be a problem with their operation. But all patients wanted to make sure they were fine, so the extra patients we saw on Tuesday were a combination of BOTH the callers and the stoics, plus new patients.

About halfway through the afternoon onslaught, Maya caught me between exam rooms and said that Mary Louise was on the phone. She usually doesn't call during work hours, so I picked up the extension right away.

"Everything all right?"

"No. Annie had to get Bob into the emergency room. He started drinking first thing this morning, then passed out and hit his head, so she called 911. She was hoping you could stop by and see him."

"I'll be happy to do so. I have another hour or two in clinic, then I can get over there."

"Okay, thanks. Sorry to bother. Love you."

I was able to go see Bob Jackson around 4 p.m. He was belligerent, as drunks often are, but seemed to calm down a bit after I arrived. He had an intravenous drip in place which carried a yellow liquid full of vitamins into the vein. His head was covered with a bloody bandage. The charge nurse, Rebecca Loftin, I knew from many visits to the ER.

"Friend of yours, Doc Brady?"

"Yes and no. His wife is my wife's childhood best friend. What's his status?"

"He came in drunk as a skunk, raising all kinds of hell. We had to restrain him, then put in the IV and started a hangover cocktail. What's his story?"

"He's always been a drinker, but more so lately, and drinking in the morning now. He's starting to pass out, get mean, become combative, the usual symptoms of alcoholism."

"Any precipitating causes, as far as you know?"

"You would have to ask the wife. She should be here."

"What does he do for a living?"

"Car dealer."

Rebecca nodded her head. "At least he doesn't have to be sober to do his job."

"Ugly, Beck, ugly."

Bob Jackson was held still in his ER bed with restraints. He appeared to be sleeping, so I gently touched his left knee. That produced a hyperkinetic response as his leg became rigid and his entire body jerked as though he was having a seizure.

"Bob, relax, it's Jim Brady. Bob? Can you hear me?"

His body collapsed as though the air had been punctured out of a balloon. He opened his eyes and stared at me. "What am I doing here?"

"Annie called 911 and the EMTs brought you in. Seems as though you lost control this morning. Looks like you and alcohol have entered a bad relationship together. What's going on?"

He teared up. "Brady, I don't know. I have a great business and a great wife, but once I get into the sauce, I just cannot quit. It's become a sickness. I guess I'll have to get help. I just want to be able to have a few drinks like my friends and enjoy the buzz. I don't want to be out of control."

"We have some good toxicologists and psychiatrists here at HCMC. They'll help you figure it out. You may have to go to a facility, though. You can be detoxified here, but most of the time folks with your problem must spend at least thirty days in a lockdown program with other people like yourself, the camaraderie of recovery and all that."

"Doesn't sound good."

"No, I wouldn't think so. You'll be missing a lot of cocktail hours, maybe for the rest of your life."

"Thanks, Brady, what a pal you are."

"Think nothing of it, Bob. From what I hear, rehab is like boot camp with a drill sergeant. You must be strong to survive. I'll research facilities in the area for you, get with Annie and Mary Louise, and get you the best help we can find."

"I don't want to lose Annie. She's the best thing I have going for me."

"You won't lose her, but you'll probably have to live your life differently."

"I'm embarrassed for my children. What will they think?"

"What other people think is not the problem right now. Getting help and getting well should be the foremost goal in your life. Besides, your kids are grown, and they know what you're like, so I suspect none of this will be a surprise to them. In fact, they'll probably be thrilled that you're reaching out for help."

"I'm not reaching anywhere with these restraints on me. Can they be removed?"

"Your doctors and nurses will make that decision. Just try to get yourself into a calm zone and let the medicos do their job. I'll check on you later, probably tomorrow."

He shook my hand, cried a bit, then nodded off to sleep.

CHAPTER 7

# THE FOURTH VICTIM

**M**ary Louise and I decided to go to the Horseshoe Bay Yacht Club for dinner. We opted for an outside table near the water. Several boats were docked nearby. Citizens who lived on Lake LBJ often took their boats to dinner and parked in docks available for just that purpose. We ordered Tito's dirty vodka martinis and toasted each other when they arrived.

"Here's to Bob Jackson," I said. "May he get to a better place in his life."

"What will happen? Annie is beside herself."

"Well, he'll get cleaned up at HCMC, then referred to an alcohol and drug rehab center, and he'll spend however much time the professionals there think he needs. It's a tough problem. The real danger is in the withdrawal portion of the treatment. The medicos here will get him through that phase. You may or may not know this, but when you've been drinking for a while and suddenly stop, you go into withdrawal. That can produce all sorts of symptoms, such as tremors, insomnia, nausea and vomiting, dehydration, and anxiety. Then the patient develops a rapid heart rate, blood pressure lability, and sometimes what is called the DTs, which is short for delirium tremens. That involves hallucinations, severe dehydration, and all sorts of cardiac problems, even death if it isn't treated."

"Oh, my. I had no idea."

"Yep. So, much better to be able to be a social drinker. Real alcoholism is a disease, and damn hard to fix."

I had soft-shell crab, and Mary Louise had a petite filet and pommes frites, also known as french fries, for the uninformed. After dinner we took a walk through the pool area and the boardwalk and found two comfortable lounge chairs behind the pool bar, the sounds of Lake LBJ water lapping at the edge being the most prominent feature.

I was just beginning to feel that wonderful moment when the stresses of the day begin to pass when my cell phone rang.

"Dr. Brady," I answered.

"Jim, it's Joan Wilcox. We have a fourth victim. I have an authorization for you to attend the crime scene, if you're available."

"Joan, I would give my eye teeth to be there, but I start surgery at 7 a.m. and I don't want to compromise my skills by being out too late."

"Jim, the crime scene is on FM 2147 at the Stop and Go. Where are you?"

"The Yacht Club, which is five minutes away."

"I'll see you there."

Mary Louise felt safer staying with me than going home alone, so we drove to the Stop and Go together. There were police and sheriff vehicles parked everywhere in the area, so it was easy to locate the crime scene. Mary Louise waited in the car while I wandered to the yellow crime-scene tape that surrounded the grocery store and gas pumps.

I told the first officer I encountered that I was Dr. Brady, and that Sheriff Joan Wilcox was expecting me. He used his radio to communicate, and shortly Joan appeared. She was dressed in her sheriff's uniform with a full utility belt and weapon and wore a small Stetson cowboy hat.

"Did Mary Louise come with you?"

"Yes, she's in the car. The black Tahoe," I said, and pointed toward the road. She walked over to the truck, had a conversation with Mary Louise I could not hear, then returned.

"Let's take a look together," she said. We walked around to the back of the store. I noticed trash cans and debris scattered about the area.

"What is it with this guy and trash?"

"We don't know yet. I assume being a surgeon and all you're not squeamish, but prepare yourself."

Several officers parted to allow us entry to the area. The crime-scene techs were present, taking photographs of a young man lying in the middle of empty containers, beer cans, and other forms of refuse. He was small and was wearing shorts, sneakers, high socks, and an orange University of Texas tee shirt.

"Turn his head this way, please," Joan asked the technician politely. He did so, and the gruesome wound that had characterized the other three murders appeared. "Tell the doctor what you told me."

"The wound starts on the left side of the cranium but was made with enough force that the killing object—we're not sure what it is but suspect it's a short axe or hatchet of some sort—went all the way through the brain pan and out the other side."

"Best guess, was the wound made with one blow or several?" I asked.

"Definitely one continuous blow, from parietal lobe to parietal lobe and out the other side. The assailant is strong and has a very sharp weapon."

"What about a wallet? Is there one, and does anything appear to be missing?"

The tech turned the victim from side to side and found there was a wallet in the rear left shorts pocket. He held up the worn leather billfold for Joan to see. She asked the tech to thumb through it while we watched. There was a small amount of cash still present, but no credit cards and no driver's license that we could see.

"Is there any form of ID in the wallet?"

The tech found a Costco card. "Assuming this is his wallet and his card, his name is Freddie Simons."

"Anything else you need to tell me?" asked Joan.

"No, ma'am, but he'll be autopsied tomorrow. We'll let you know if anything different turns up in comparison to the other murders. To me, this pattern looks the same as the others. We'll work on locating next of kin with whichever one of your detectives you assign to the case."

Joan took my arm and walked me back to the car. "What do you think?"

"No idea. I looked through the files you gave me, and on my initial review I didn't see anything of significance in common other than the method of killing. Now we have four missing driver's licenses. I think that I'll have to eventually interview the families of the victims. Is that allowed?"

"Well, yes. My detectives did that initially but came up with nothing. I see no reason why you can't talk to them again, although I don't think you'll get far, especially with Bart Smalls's parents. The Berry family might be of more help since it was their daughter who was murdered. Hubert Brown was sort of a recluse except for his job and didn't have a relationship with any of his children or grandchildren, according to the ex-wife. And Delores

White's only relative is a mother with dementia who's past reliable communication."

Mary Louise and I ventured home, walked Tip, and had a glass of wine in bed so we could sleep.

"Was it bad? The scene?"

"Horrible. That is the fourth life snuffed out in the same horrifying manner."

"Will you be able to sleep?"

"I think so."

"I want to feel close to you," Mary Louise said. She arose from the bed, removed her underwear and tee shirt, crawled back into bed, and nestled against me.

"That reminds me of that old Carpenters song," I said, as my hands began to wander.

"I want to feel the love, not make love. There is a difference."

"You'll have to tell that to Little Johnny. He has other things in mind."

She ran her hand across my tumescent self. "Oh my. We cannot let that go to waste."

And we did not.

Wednesday and Thursday were repeats of Monday and Tuesday, a packed surgery schedule and an onslaught for an office day. After clinic hours were done Thursday, I called Dr. Jerry Reed, the county coroner and chief of pathology at HCMC.

"I know why you're calling me. Sheriff Joan Wilcox said to expect it. She let you get involved in these four murders, although I find that hard to believe, Brady."

"I can tell you it was a surprise to me as well. I was invited to the scene of the most recent murder last night. That wound is frightening to see up close and in person."

"Well, I've now had four of them to review, and it doesn't get any better. What can I do for you?"

"Did Joan tell you about the missing driver's licenses?"

"Yes, she did. Are you trying to think of reasons why cash and credit cards would be left behind, but the victims' driver's licenses are missing?"

"Yes, I am. Any ideas?"

"I am but the humble pathologist, not a Detective First Grade with the Burnet County Sheriff's Department."

"But yet?"

"I have an idea or two, although they might be far-fetched. My first guess would be that often, or so I have read, serial killers keep a memento of their crimes from each victim, to relive the killing experience. The Texas DL has a small picture on it, and that could be what the killer gets off to repeatedly."

"That sounds reasonable. I even considered that when I looked through the files. What else?"

"This is more far-fetched, but what if these murders represent contract killings, disguised as serial killings to keep suspicion off someone or something important? That would be quite a twist, don't you think, Brady?"

"Yes. I think Joan and I discussed a situation like that as well, but you're right—that would be way out of the ordinary. And what motive could there possibly be? These four people, as far as I know, did not know each other or have anything remotely in common. I can't imagine what the common thread would be, if there even is one."

"Something hidden, something secret. Maybe the victims didn't know they had something in common with each other. It would be fun to figure that out, but I have a real job."

"I have a real job also, Jerry. But I'm making time to help Joan out with this investigation."

"And that is good for you, my friend. I'll assist in any way possible."

"Did you do a tox screen on the victims?"

"Yes. The first three came back, and there was nothing to report. I just sent this week's victim's blood samples off. It takes a week or so, sometimes longer, to get the results."

"Man, four dead people, negative tox screen in three, no motives, no clues."

"Now you see why the good Sheriff Joan asked you for help."

"I would love to get Susan Beeson involved. This is a perfect case for her, don't you think?"

"She certainly has been helpful in the past. I would be honored to work with her again. She shut those organized-crime assholes down for that La Cava Golf Club business, that's for sure, and got Devlin and Savolio each healthy prison terms. That could not have happened to a nicer bunch of guys."

"I have to say, I think Sheriff Joan called me in, thinking I might want to get Susan involved, but that I would perhaps do that on the QT such that the feds would not take over her case."

"Jim Bob, that will not happen. I don't know ASAC Beeson as well as you do, but once you call her in, she'll arrive like a freight train on a nonstop track. Lock and load: that seems to be her motto."

"Amen to that, Jerry."

# CHAPTER 8

# THE FBI ARRIVES

I had employed Maya Stern as my administrative assistant for a few years, and while she was excellent at her job and great in dealing with people, I hated—for reasons I could not explain—to involve her in the task at hand, that of looking for hidden similarities between the recent murder victims. At the same time, I didn't have the time to work, play golf, and gather information about the crimes without help, so . . . I got her involved.

Belinda and I made rounds routinely at 8 a.m. on Friday morning, unless an emergency had come in on Thursday night that required surgery. Thankfully there were no emergency admissions for me, so after rounds were completed, we, as a courtesy, ventured onto the psych ward, a small, locked-down unit designed to care for the mentally and emotionally challenged, in order to visit with Bob Jackson. Outside the locked ward was an intercom, which Belinda buzzed. The celestial voice said "Yes?" I stated our desire to see Mr. Jackson, and we presented our respective IDs to the photo scanner adjacent to the intercom. We were buzzed in and directed to Room 4. I counted only twelve rooms in the unit, each a private room and each apparently locked from the outside, each with a screen over the glass window that looked onto each patient's bed.

"How is he?" I asked the nurse that accompanied us into Bob's room.

"He seems to be enjoying his Librium cocktail. With the history his wife gave us, I was worried about him slipping into DTs, but that didn't happen. He's been tame, compared to his behavior documented by the admitting ER staff."

"Do you know what the plan is?"

"The wife is meeting with the staff psychiatrist today, so we shall see."

Bob was sleeping soundly. I started to try and wake him, then remembered the adage about letting sleeping dogs lie. I thanked the nurse for her time, and Belinda and I returned to the clinic building. I asked Maya to come into my office.

"I haven't done anything wrong, have I, Dr. Brady? I so love this job, and I can't—"

"Maya, your job performance is commendable. You've done nothing wrong. You're an exemplary employee, and I'm proud to have you as part of the team."

"Oh, I was so afraid when you called this morning and said you wanted to meet. I thought you might be firing me."

"Maya, I see you and I working together as long as we both want to work. This is about something else, something off the books, so to speak. You probably know that I get involved in investigating murders and acts of mayhem and assorted mysteries from time to time. It's a passion of mine, and I have a knack for discovery, and sometimes I see in a situation what no one else sees, and therefore I can be valuable to law enforcement."

"Yes, sir, I do."

"Good. Well, I am involved in a case, and I need help . . . from you."

"Anything, Dr. Brady. I am at your service, sir."

I explained to her about the four murdered victims with their heads bashed open, and about our few pitiful theories as to the reasons for the crimes that Jerry Reed and I had discussed.

"I don't exactly get what it is you want me to do."

"I'm looking for threads of a relationship between the victims, and therefore we—meaning you—must contact the families, set up appointments for me to interview them, and research their lives to see what we can find. I need you to make that happen."

"You mean like call the relatives, set up interview times, maybe even ask questions that might lead you in a certain direction to determine whether these killings are related in some way and not just a series of random serial killings?"

"Maya, I think you have it down. I'll give you the contact information on the four victims and see what you can arrange. I acknowledge that I might have to give up golf on a Friday or Saturday to visit with these folks, but that's fine. I will be at your disposal. If you need extra compensation for the extra work . . ."

"Dr. Brady, no extra payment is necessary. I'm honored to help. Besides, as you know, when my lovely Aunt Patsy was murdered as part of the Devlin matter, I came into a large sum of money and inherited her beautiful home. I'm working here for the joy of it, and am ready, willing, and able to assist you, sir. Now, about those names and phone numbers . . ."

Maya made copies of the files that Joan Wilcox shared with me, then asked if she would be able to call the sheriff for further information about the victims and their relatives if the paperwork was incomplete. I told her I would assume so but would call Joan and verify, which I did while still at the office.

"So, now MY help is getting HIS OWN help?" Joan asked.

"Maya is trustworthy and efficient. I don't have the time to set up meetings with the families, so she's handling that part of my duties. And, if she happens to discover something in your files that leads us in a positive direction toward finding the killer, even better. She will not share the information with anyone, I can assure you. I'm trying to help you out best I can, but I need help with the legwork and phone calls."

"I trust you, and you trust Maya, so we're just a happy little band of trusting people. Keep in touch."

I completed the required paperwork on my desk, bid adieu to Maya and Belinda, and headed to the golf course. I had an hour before my tee time and reasoned I would have plenty of time to warm up and get a sandwich before teeing off. I took my usual route, west on Highway 71, then doubled back to FM 2147 and traveled east to Club Drive and drove up the winding hill to Horseshoe Bay Golf Club. Before I reached the club, a large pickup truck came out of nowhere off to my right, requiring me to swerve left, almost driving me into a large limestone wall separating the inbound and outbound lanes. I slammed on the brakes as hard as possible to prevent contact with either the truck or the wall. I stopped just before I crashed into the truck, which had one of those giant metal grill guards that would prevent an injury to the truck's front end, but which would enhance the damage to my front fender and engine block.

The driver wore a ball cap pulled down low, almost over his eyes, and wore sunglasses. I was close enough to his driver's seat to read a logo on the cap, which was SUPPORT BCSD. The driver gave me the universal sign of greeting with his middle finger and sped away. My paranoia got the best of me, and I called the Burnet County sheriff's office and asked to speak to Sheriff Wilcox.

"Solved the case already?" she asked, after the requisite minute or so of my waiting on hold.

"No, but a few minutes ago I was almost run over by a massive truck driven by a man wearing a cap with the logo SUPPORT BCSD. Would that be one of yours?"

She hesitated for long enough that I knew the answer was yes. "Probably."

"And the letters stand for Burnet County Sheriff's Department, right?"

"Correct."

"I have to suspect that one of your detectives is not happy that I'm reviewing his cases."

"Well, yes, but all the members of the department have the caps. Plus, we had a fundraiser earlier in the year. We gave out those caps for a $100 donation. Lots of folks bought those hats, Jim Bob. It could have been anybody. I don't think anyone on my staff would pull a stunt like that."

"Well, he gave me the middle finger salute, so I would not be too sure about that, Joan," I said, and hung up.

I had a beer with lunch to calm my nerves after the truck encounter. One of the problems with a doctor being a part-time investigator is that I really had no standing. There was no badge, no weapon, no credentials to equalize me to established law enforcement. I was just out there on my own with no real backup other than, in this case, the word of the sheriff who, for all practical purposes, was unable to follow me around to make sure I didn't get injured. I had already experienced the runner in the dog park, and who knew what that meant. Now I potentially had a deputy sheriff after me, probably because he was mad that I was reviewing his work. I expected I was going to get it from all sides.

As a result of my anxiety, I played a crappy round of golf and lost money. I picked up my cell phone to call Mary Louise to tell her I was on the way home, then remembered Friday was her day to go to Austin for charity board work. I noticed two messages on my phone, one from her, and one from Maya requesting a call-back.

"I'll pick up steaks for dinner if you don't mind firing up the grill. Love you," said the recorded Mary Louise.

"I made appointments for you to talk to two families tomorrow," Maya said when I called her back. "I'm working on the others. Unfortunately, the two interviews are in the morning, so I apologize if that interferes with your golf game."

"Not a problem. Who am I seeing tomorrow?"

"At 9 a.m. you'll talk to Hubert Brown's ex-wife. At noon, Noni Berry's family. I've emailed you all the info you'll need—addresses, phone numbers, and a synopsis of the findings at the time of death."

"What about the family of Bart Smalls? Were they cooperative?"

She laughed. "Not only no, but hell no. Rude people. I heard loud heavy-metal rock in the background, and the father was slurring his words. He wanted to know how much we could pay him to have a meeting. Good luck with talking to those people. I thought the son was the driver of the car but not the victim. Why would you want to talk with him?"

"Not sure, really. Maybe for completeness's sake. He was inside the store when she was killed in the parking lot."

"I see. Well, I think it'll be a waste of time if you have to get involved with his parents to talk to him. Bart is eighteen years old. He can speak to you on his own if he chooses. Maybe you can talk to the other three victims' families first, then talk to him as a last resort."

"All right, Maya, thanks much. It sounds like you're getting into this. That's good. Talk to you later."

I called Chuck, the Saturday game organizer, and told him I was unable to play the next day due to some investigative work I was doing. He knew what kind of prying-into-people's-lives I did in my spare time.

"Good, although I don't know why you continue sticking your nose into matters that are not your concern. I had twenty-five signed up so I was going to have to get someone to sit out. We can't play fivesomes on Saturdays as you know, so I have an even number now."

"Which is all you really care about, Chuck. It doesn't matter who's playing as long as it's an even number."

"You want to run this group, Brady? I'll be happy to turn it over to you."

"Not on your life, Chuck. I don't need another thankless job."

I got home at five thirty, opened a beer, and fed and walked Tip. Just as I sat in a recliner on the terrace, I heard Mary Louise's car in the driveway. That was my signal to start the grill.

"Anybody home?" she yelled from the kitchen.

"Yep. Just starting the grill."

I walked inside once the grill was lit, and I noticed a different fragrance in the house. Tip barked once, a dog signal of some sort. I heard the toilet flush, and around the corner came, to my surprise, our old friend Susan Beeson, assistant special agent in charge at the Austin FBI.

"Surprise," she said. "From the look on your face, Mary Louise didn't tell you I was coming for dinner."

"No, but it's not a problem. Always great to see you," I said, as we hugged. Mary Louise walked out of the bedroom about that time.

"Something going on between you two?"

"You know she's not my type, Mary Louise. Look at her. Nice jacket, pressed white shirt, tan khakis, and all ruined by those brown orthopedic shoes."

"You have a problem with my orthopedic shoes? They're comfortable, and as much as I'm on my feet all day, I need the support."

"It isn't so much orthopedic shoes as it is . . . the style. Okay, it is the orthopedic shoes. I'm just thinking you might consider another style that's just as supportive but maybe less . . . oh hell, what do I know? I think you ladies need a beverage."

I prepared Tito's dirty vodka martinis with regular olives for me and bleu-cheese olives for Susan and Mary Louise. We toasted and went out to the terrace to enjoy the transition to early evening.

"Are you here on a case, Susan?"

"Yes."

"Can you discuss it?"

"I can because you already know about it. In fact, our mutual friend Sheriff Joan Wilcox got me involved. I believe you're tasked with reviewing the investigating detectives' work, are you not? And did you not call her this morning and suggest that one of her D's might have tried to run your truck off the road?"

"Yes, but—"

"Joan is a smart woman and knows you could be in over your head. It's one thing to have you going around interviewing relatives of murdered folk, not knowing whether they could possibly be involved or not. But it's another bag of worms to think that a detective might have targeted you because you could possibly step on their toes. So, I'm here to be your . . . companion, if you will."

"Bodyguard sounds more like it. Maya set up two interviews for tomorrow."

"Then I shall accompany you and assume the role of secretary during these interviews."

"Seriously, you're going to sit in on interviews and not tell these relatives you're the ASAC of the Austin FBI? Is that not subterfuge of some sort?"

"Yes. Yes, it is. But think of me in different terms, perhaps as a weaponized note taker, present to keep the peace."

She and Mary Louise both smiled. Not one, not two, but now three women looking after me. How could anything possibly go wrong?

# CHAPTER 9

# INTERVIEWS, PART 1

**H**ubert Brown had lived in Highland Haven, a small community on the north side of the Colorado River. His home was single story and sat on a small canal that eventually fed into Lake LBJ. The house was run-down and needed paint, as did the small boat dock. No boat was present in the dock. The yard was poorly maintained, with weeds above ankle high. That put me on edge, looking out for pesky rattlesnakes. Getting intimate with a cottonmouth snake was not in my plans for the day. Fortunately, I had worn a pair of old elephant-skin boots, so I was protected as much as one could be against those slithering sidewinders. Susan, on the other hand, had on the same pair of brown shoes as the day before, which didn't even cover her ankles.

"Tread carefully, Susan. This is snake country."

"Snakes? I hate snakes." She started looking around at the ground, hopping in little steps back toward the truck.

About that time, an older Chevy sedan pulled into the driveway. A woman with mahogany skin exited the car and walked toward me. She looked to be in her mid-fifties and was dressed in hospital scrubs. She had short hair, almost a buzz cut, stippled with gray, and had a broad smile.

"I'm Lizzie Brown. Are you Dr. Brady?"

"Yes, ma'am. Thank you so much for meeting me. My assistant Susan is in the car. When I mentioned snakes, she ran."

She laughed. "You're right about those snakes. I cannot tell you how many I have killed on the riding lawnmower we used to have."

"Are you a nurse?"

"Yes, sir, I work at HCMC."

"I do as well, and I don't remember seeing you around."

"The hospital has become so large I hardly know the other workers these days. I know who you are, though. You have quite the reputation."

"That could be good or bad."

"All good, Dr. Brady. Your reputation is that of a great surgeon and the patients think you walk on water."

"You're too kind. I think that Maya called you and set up this appointment."

"Yes, she's such a dear and so kind. She told me you were appointed by the sheriff of Burnet County to investigate Hubie's murder, and that you wanted to meet me and see if I had any information that might help in the investigation."

"That is correct. Let me get Susan out of the car. Maybe we could go inside and sit?"

I introduced Lizzie Brown to my "assistant" Susan. We went inside the house, which was warm. Lizzie turned on the window air conditioner, went into the kitchen, and prepared iced tea for us.

"I get the impression that you're familiar with the house, and kept in touch with Mr. Brown?"

"Oh, yes, I lived here with Hubie for quite a few years. We raised our three kids in this house. When we got divorced, I went to live in Kingsland with my parents who had been getting up in years. My father passed, and my mother was not well, so I just stayed there. Mama eventually passed as well, and I inherited the house. It's only ten minutes away."

"I see. I imagine you've heard the details of Mr. Brown's murder. He was killed in the rear area behind a grocery-gas station he frequented on the way to work at HCMC. The authorities have no clues, and no motive whatsoever for his killing. Their best guess is a random murder, perhaps by a serial killer, since nothing was taken from his wallet as far as they know, other than his driver's license."

She was pensive for a moment. "I never liked that store. I wanted him to find someplace else on his route to the hospital, but he always had to stop and get his goodie bag for work, and he liked that old place. It wasn't a chain, and that was important to him. He always tried to use the 'mom and pop' stores. You know, Doc, x-ray technicians on the night shift are usually like Hubie, quiet and not much on interacting with folks. He had a lot of spare time on his shift and read quite a bit. I just can't believe he's gone."

"It sounds like you were still close?"

"Oh, yes. I never remarried, neither did he. We loved each other but just could not live with each other. You know? I mean, not to speak ill of the dead, but Hubie had his problems. Mentally, I mean."

"Do you have any ideas about who might have wanted him dead? Or anything about his past that might have prompted his murder?"

"No, sir. I've thought about it for the past three months, and for the life of me, I cannot think of a thing."

"You mentioned mental problems. What was that about?"

She sighed and stared at the floor. Susan looked at me and shrugged her shoulders.

"He was diagnosed as having bipolar disorder. He would get these spells and go wild, the manic part of bipolar, then get into a deep depression so bad he couldn't work. It was terrible. He got so bad one night I had to call 911. That had to be about ten years ago or so. The kids were all grown by that time and had moved out. He went so wild I thought he was going to kill me. The ambulance took him to a small hospital in Marble Falls. This is before HCMC was completed. The Marble Falls hospital couldn't deal with him, so then they took him to a hospital in Austin, a mental hospital of some sort. He was there for three months, and when he came out, he was a changed man. I wasn't allowed to see him while he was there, which I thought was a bad thing, but he turned over a new leaf and all those symptoms just went away."

"Do you remember the name of the hospital?"

"It's been so long, I don't. I can look through his records and let you know if I find something."

"Thanks. Do you know what kind of treatment he had there?"

"He said shock treatments and some kind of medication."

"And he never had the symptoms again?"

"No, sir, not that I ever saw."

"Did he stay on the medication?"

"Yes. He kept his pill bottles in the bathroom. Let me see if that particular medication is still there. I'll be right back."

"What do you think, Susan?" I asked, as Lizzie exited the room.

"I think that you should give an instructional class to my young agents on how to interview a witness. You are brilliant."

I felt myself turn red from the compliment. Fortunately, Lizzie returned with a small brown bottle of capsules.

"Here you go, Doc Brady. He took one a day for all these years."

"I don't recognize the medication by name, but this is probably a generic. May I take it with me?"

"Of course. Hubie won't be needing them any longer," she said, and started to cry.

"We'll see ourselves out. You've been a great help. Thank you so much."

Lizzie Brown reached up and gave me a hug. "Thanks for caring about Hubie. I appreciate it more than you know."

"I don't remember seeing any medical records in any of those victims' files. Can you check that, Susan?"

She researched the data that we had in our possession on the drive to the Berry family residence. "Nothing about medical history for any of the victims. But I don't think evaluating the past medical conditions of people murdered by an axe to the head would be foremost in any investigator's mind, Jim Bob."

"Maybe not, Susan, but we have new information about Hubert Brown, and researching that aspect might possibly lead us to something; what, we do not know. Could be a dead end, could be important."

"I'll make a notation to check medical histories on the four victims," Susan said.

Noni Berry had lived with her parents in a nice home on the water near the Ferguson Power Plant on the south end of Lake LBJ. The house was a two-story, with a beautiful wraparound deck on the first floor. There was a customized boat dock with two slots, containing a speed boat in one and a pontoon boat in the other.

Noni Berry's mother greeted us at the door. After the introduction, she invited us in and led us to a great room with a spectacular view of Lake LBJ. The power plant, while a massive structure, could not be seen from the rear of the house. Apparently, the developers had realized early on that if they wanted to sell houses on the water in this location, the plant would have to be hidden from the view corridor.

As far as I could tell, we three were alone in the house. Noni's mother, first name Trish, was still in a fragile emotional state due to the loss of her daughter, and she held a box of tissues in her hand. She sat in a wingback chair, and we took a small sofa across a coffee table from her.

"Your secretary Maya was so kind on the phone and said you needed to ask me some questions about Noni. She said you were doing interviews of the victims' families at the request of Sheriff Wilcox."

"Yes, that's correct. She was eighteen years old?"

"Yes, and her life was snuffed out because of Bart Smalls."

"Why do you say that?"

"Well, he was driving the car and had stopped at the store to get munchies for after they got high. You know, pot makes you hungry."

"Yes, I do. Was your daughter in the habit of getting high with Bart?"

"Unfortunately, yes. He was her downfall. We raised her better than that, but after a certain age, there's nothing a parent can do. Noni had always been on the unstable side, emotionally."

"Was she on any kind of medication, or had she seen a psychiatrist or been hospitalized for emotional problems?"

Trish nodded her head and abruptly stood and left the room. She returned with a handful of pill bottles. "Take your pick."

She handed me six bottles, each containing capsules or tablets. "She was taking all these pills?"

"Not all of them and not every day. The doctors had educated her on the effects of each drug and had tried to teach her which ones to take, depending on how her mood swings were on any given day. It was complicated, but she was a smart girl and had been doing well for the past year. Except for Bart Smalls, who is just as guilty as the actual murderer, if you ask me."

"I need to get an evaluation of these medications. May I take them with me?"

"Of course. What need do I have for them now?" she said, and started to wail.

Susan got up from the sofa, wedged herself next to Trish, and held her for a moment until she calmed down.

"Just one more question, Trish, and we'll be on our way. Had Noni ever been hospitalized for her mental problems?"

"Yes, one time, about two years ago."

"And where was that, if you don't mind telling me."

"A hospital in Austin that specialized in Noni's kind of problems."

"What was their diagnosis?"

"The doctors said she was bipolar. It used to be called manic-depression."

"And do you remember the name of the hospital she was admitted to?"

"Yes. Blue Lake Psychiatric Hospital."

CHAPTER 10

# PARTY

I had missed my golf game, so I called Mary Louise on the cell and asked if she wanted to meet Susan and me for a late lunch. We decided on Bay View Restaurant and Bar, high atop a hill overlooking Lake LBJ and Lake Marble Falls. It had recently been remodeled and opened under a new name with new ownership.

It was by then two o'clock in the afternoon. We sat outside under a massive oak tree at a redwood table with superb water views. We each opted for a Bloody Mary, and I ordered an appetizer of peel-and-eat shrimp to share.

"How did the morning go?" Mary Louise asked.

"Your husband is a natural at the interview process. He is brilliant, simply brilliant. He gives the interviewee a level of comfort that allows him to ask the hard questions. It was a joy to watch."

I felt myself turning red again but was rescued by the arrival of drinks and food. I ordered a shrimp po' boy and both Mary Louise and Susan ordered the shrimp salad.

"What's next?" asked Mary Louise.

"We need to interview the next two victims' families, those of Delores White and Freddie Simons. And I'll have to research mental illness and treatment medications. Turns out both Noni Berry and Hubert Brown were on meds for bipolar disorder."

"I told him that the fact that two of the victims were on psych meds may not have anything whatsoever to do with their murders. But we must follow the leads, wherever they take us," said Susan.

After lunch, we three headed back to our house for a post-prandial nap. I was asleep almost before my head hit the pillow. I reasoned that investigative work was stressful and required plenty of rest to do the job justice.

I awoke to the sound of my cell phone buzzing, looked at the message, and saw that Maya had sent me a text. It read *call me please*, which I did.

"So sorry to bother you, Dr. Brady, but I wondered if I had made a mistake by setting up the last two interviews for Sunday?"

"Well, not really. I have no plans for tomorrow. Mary Louise and I usually play couples golf, but we can miss a day."

"Delores White was said to have no relatives other than her mother with dementia, who lived with her. But I was able to track down an aunt who seemed mentally intact, at least over the phone, and she is willing to meet you at 10 a.m. tomorrow morning at the coffee shop where her niece worked. I was able to locate Freddie Simons's father as well, and he can meet you at noon at his home in Marble Falls."

"Maya, I am amazed at your tenacity. Good job. I'll see you Monday, and thanks again."

"Who was that?" asked Mary Louise, as she stirred from our late-afternoon siesta.

"Maya. She set up two interviews for tomorrow. I know it's Sunday and all, and our day for golf, but I wanted to get these out of the way."

"Not a problem. Besides, we'll probably be out late tonight and not be in the mood for much physical activity."

"What is tonight?"

She leaned up on one elbow and said, "You don't remember?"

"No, sorry."

"Del Andersen's party, the one she is giving mostly in your honor for keeping your word and giving her and *The Highlander* the scoop in the Devlin business last year."

"Oh, man, I completely forgot. I am not in the mood. I just want to laze around, maybe see if I can make some inroads into parts of your anatomy."

"As nice as that would be, it's already 5 p.m. and your wife has to look her best. You jump in the shower first, then leave me to the complicated process of looking ten years younger than my age."

Del Andersen was the owner, chair of the board, and chief editor of *The Highlander*, our local newspaper. I had replaced her hip last year, and Del was a grateful patient, as well as a social friend and fellow board member of HCMC. I had promised her a first look at the mess Louis Devlin and his alleged Kansas City underworld colleagues had made of La Cava Golf Estates. Her articles scooped all the big locals, the Austin paper as well as the Dallas and Houston papers, on reporting the scheme, and as a result she was up for awards from her peers.

I dressed for the occasion in black jeans, black ostrich boots, and a colorful silk Tommy Bahama shirt.

Mary Louise emerged from her boudoir looking at least ten years younger than her age. She wore a black cashmere sweater, black slacks with a billowy hem, and black open-toed sandals with heels. Her hair was done partially up in a complicated 'do with small pieces of turquoise jewelry interspersed among the curls.

"Wow. You look like an ad in *Texas Monthly* magazine."

"For what?"

"Excuse me?"

"I look like an ad for what kind of product?"

"Oh. Cheesecake, maybe?"

"That was the perfect answer. Let us depart, boyfriend," she said, as she sashayed by me. Her scent was dizzying, but I was able to overcome my emotions and carry on.

Del lived in a beautiful home on Island Drive in Horseshoe Bay. She had arranged for valet parking, which was a blessing on the long, narrow street. From the entry point, houses on Island Drive didn't look like much. However, the lots were dramatically pie-shaped, so when we entered and stepped into a great room, water seemed to surround the place. Del greeted us and was dressed in a pantsuit of creamy white and had on matching sandals with rhinestones on the toe straps. Her hair looked to have been professionally done, and she was aglow.

"Thanks for coming, you two." She air-kissed us both and directed us to the bar, which was set up outside on the wraparound concrete deck. The waters of Lake LBJ lapped two feet below the deck. The lake view was about a 270-degree arc. Del had a pontoon boat in the boat slip nearby with a captain who was offering rides to the patrons. There was a healthy breeze that evening, so most takers of the boat ride were men, the women preferring to preserve their hairstyles for the evening.

A trio consisting of a female singer and two guitar players was set up on the corner of the neighbors' adjacent concrete deck, so I assumed those residents were either not at home or were part of the festivities. The band was playing their version of light classic rock and country tunes, and they were quite talented, as would be expected with all the musicians available in the Austin area for parties.

"Good evening to the Brady family," said Dr. Buck Owens, founder and chair of the board of Hill Country Medical Center. He was shorter than me by a few inches, and he had his gray hair cut military short. He shook my hand and attempted to steal a smooch from Mary Louise, but she was adept at avoiding such invasions of privacy and turned her head at the last minute, such that our friend Buck merely grazed an ear with his puckered lips.

"Quite a place, huh?" Buck said.

"Beautiful. We looked at a few lakefront properties when we bought here," I said, "but we preferred to be on one of the hills above the lake. The distant view worked better for us, especially when it came to the summer bug invasion. Your place is on the water as I remember, Buck. You must like the view from here as well."

"Brady, if you want to have easy access to a boat for fishing or cruising, or whatever, you have to be on the water."

"Buck, I guess Mary Louise and I favor looking at the water, not being in or on the water."

"Your loss. I need to mix and mingle. See you later."

"He is a testy little man, Jim Bob."

"He really is a good guy, and generous; probably just needs a woman in his life to soften him up a bit, don't you think?"

"Maybe soften, maybe harden, depending on the circumstances," she said, and stared at me with that come-hither look she had, one of many in her armamentarium designed to melt me into a soft buttery mass.

I reached for her rear end, but she deflected my hand gracefully, whispered, "Later, gator," and strolled off to visit acquaintances.

I saw an old friend, Madeline O'Rourke, known affectionately to us as Sister Mads. A former nun, she ran Mourning Doves, a women's shelter providing temporary food, clothing, and housing for the abused and downtrodden. Mary Louise and I were on the board of her facility. She did great work for the community.

"You're looking handsome this evening, Doc," she said, as she gave me a chaste hug.

"You as well, Mads." She was not much of a dresser normally, but she had on an attractive blouse, nice slacks, and low heels, so it appeared to me that someone might have assisted her with her wardrobe. Her gray hair was as always cut in a pixie, making her seem even smaller than her frame of barely five feet.

"I hear through the grapevine that you're helping out our new sheriff with what could be a serial killer in our midst."

"How in the world could you possibly know about that?"

"I have my eyes, ears, and nose to the ground always, young man. You probably haven't discovered this tidbit yet, but one of the victims, Delores White, was one of my girls years ago."

"You mean a temporary resident, or a worker bee?"

"A resident. Her old man was a bad one, he was."

"You mean husband, or father?"

"Husband. She's been divorced from him for years, but he was able to do some damage to that poor child back in the day . . . broke a few bones, gave her a few concussions and such. She had a hard life. As I remember, her mother has dementia of some variety, and Delores was trying to care for her at home and still work to support them both. Bless her heart, she could never catch a break. And now this. Have you spoken to her mother?"

"That is on my agenda for tomorrow. Maya, my admin assistant, tracked down Delores's aunt. I was originally told that Delores had no relatives other than her mother, but fortunately there is someone who can answer questions about Delores that hopefully has a relatively clear head."

"H-mmm. I don't remember an aunt, but it has been a while since Delores White was part of my life. Anyway, good luck with those interviews." Sister Mads reached up and patted my cheek and walked away. She had reminded me of what a small world we lived in.

Mary Louise returned to my side. "Hungry?"

"Yes. You?"

"Starved. Del had Opie's BBQ cater the event. I have been smelling their delicious pork ribs since we arrived."

We joined the buffet line, loaded our plates with ribs, brisket, jalapeño sausage, potato salad, and beans with bacon, then slathered the plate with barbeque sauce. Because Del had the event catered, there were adequate chairs and tables provided for the patrons to sit. She probably had appreciated the difficulty in trying to balance a plate of barbecue on one's lap. Once everyone was seated and the noise had died down, Del stepped up to one of the band member's microphones.

"Thanks to y'all for coming to my little shindig. I want to brag a little about two things. One is to thank my good friend and excellent orthopedic surgeon Jim Bob Brady for fixing my hip. I have a new lease on life, with no pain, and I'm grateful every day for your skill."

A little applause followed.

"Second, kudos again to Dr. Brady for uncovering the disastrous mess created by Louis Devlin and his associates in the La Cava Golf Estates project. He promised me exclusive rights to the story early on and kept his word. *The Highlander* was able to shut out the *Austin American-Statesman*, the *Houston Chronicle*, and *The Dallas Morning News* for five days, a lifetime in the newspaper business. As a result, drum roll please, I was nominated for and recently won a Peabody Award for Excellence in Journalism."

At that announcement, everyone stood and clapped loudly, barbecue sauce be damned.

"So, thanks again to all my friends for your support of our local paper all these years. Eat, drink, and do some dancin'!"

With that, the band cranked up the sound and played "Boot Scootin' Boogie" by Ronnie Dunn of Brooks & Dunn. The dance floor was on the neighbors' portion of the concrete deck, and despite the lack of space, all present crowded together and enjoyed the music.

Mary Louise and I danced for over an hour and tired ourselves out. We decided that going home earlier rather than later would be a good idea. We said goodbye to our host, walked to the valet stand, and retrieved our truck. It was only a fifteen-minute drive or so to Granite Falls, but we had to travel through the city of Horseshoe Bay to get there, and their police officers did not look kindly at drunk drivers. We rolled down the windows and carefully drove the forty-five mile-per-hour speed limit all the way home. We didn't encounter any Smokies on the way, for which we were grateful.

We arrived at our enclave and I activated the transponder to open the gate. I waited for the entry gate to shut before pressing the garage door activator. Just as I was going to pull into the garage, I saw a flash past my driver's door. It was a small person, and they tried to open the driver's door. Mary Louise screamed. I sat on the horn to make some noise. Whoever it was ran toward the entry gate and scaled it like it was nothing.

"What in the hell was that?"

"I don't know. Well, I might have an idea. I saw them the other day when I was walking Tip."

"It looked to me like whoever it was wanted to get at you. Does this have anything to do with these interviews you're doing?"

"Possibly. Get my weapon, just in case."

We each kept a pistol and permit in our respective cars for emergencies. Mary Louise got my gun from the glove compartment as I pulled into the garage, and she handed it to me as we exited from the vehicle slowly and carefully. I then extended my firearm into the shooting position and she stayed close as we walked onto the driveway. We saw and heard nothing that seemed to be a threat. We had installed outdoor flood lights that were activated by movement, such that we could see into the nooks and crannies surrounding the four yards that were protected by the large entry gate. We waited a moment for the lights to go off, then entered the house through the garage, closed the garage door, and deactivated the alarm.

Tip was glad to see us. I took him into the backyard for his last bathroom trip of the day. I kept my weapon at my side until he was done. I brought him back in, then sat in a deck chair for a moment. I had seen the flash of a person twice now and didn't know what it meant but reasoned it probably had to do with the interviews I was doing. Once again, I found myself in a situation that could produce bodily harm to either myself or Mary Louise. She would be very unhappy about that.

I had hoped for an amorous evening upon our return, but when I entered the bedroom, the lights were off and Mary Louise was under the covers with her back to me, her clothing in a pile on the floor. I completed my nighttime ablutions, quietly crawled under the covers, and stared at the ceiling until I nodded off.

CHAPTER 11

# INTERVIEWS, PART 2

"**W**ould you like to accompany Susan and me on the interviews today? You and I usually spend Sundays together, and although we wouldn't be playing golf, we'd have the day together."

We were sitting at the kitchen bar, sipping coffee and finishing off the last of the breakfast tacos we'd made. Mary Louise had scrambled the eggs, while I had chopped up shallots, red and green peppers, and black olives. She had mixed the veggies into the eggs, added sharp cheddar cheese, and cooked the mixture until the cheese had melted. We then dipped portions onto warm flour tortillas, rolled them, and added picante sauce.

"I know we had an agreement many years ago when we married, that no matter what happens, we do NOT go to bed angry. I broke the rule, and I am sorry. But that figure, or whatever it was, frightened me, and I know in some way that person is connected to the files you're reviewing of recently murdered people. You're involved, and that puts you at risk. And that scares me and angers me, because I don't know what I would do if something happened to you."

"Listen, I'm looking at the files as a favor to Joan Wilcox as you know, and interviewing folks that might have a clue as to why these murders have occurred. That's the extent of my involvement. Susan Beeson is right there during the interviews and is looking out for me. Once I have made any inroads into the whys, or even if I strike out, the case goes back to the detectives that work for Joan, and I am out. She will probably get the FBI officially involved, and Susan will take over these cases personally. This is a temporary situation."

"What I want to know is who, and what, is that person we saw last night?"

"Not a clue, Mary Louise. I'll file a report with the Granite Falls Police Department this morning. What do you say? About the interviews?"

"Okay. I'll get dressed. Do you mind cleaning up?"

"Not a bit."

Tip helped me clean up. He loved eggs and cheese wrapped in tortillas. I saw him swallow, but never saw him chew. I guessed that was unnecessary for dogs.

Susan had spent Friday night with us but had moved to the luxurious Horseshoe Bay Resort when her husband Gene joined her for a two- or- three-day vacation. She had agreed to meet me at the coffee shop where Delores White had worked.

We made the trek to the northern end of Marble Falls, almost to the southern end of the town of Burnet, and located Bubba's Diner. It would have been an insult to diners to describe Bubba's as such; it wasn't even a coffee shop. The word "dive" came to mind as we entered the facility, which smelled of fried grease and burned coffee. There was a counter with ten seats facing the kitchen, and behind that a series of eight tables which could each hold two people comfortably. There were two men sitting at the bar who may have been unhoused. Otherwise, the place was empty except for a wizened older woman with unkempt gray hair sitting alone at the far end of the row of tables. I approached her.

"Mrs. White?"

"Dr. Brady?"

"Yes, ma'am."

"White was my niece's name. I'm Livingston. Sarah Livingston."

Susan and Mary Louise had opted to stay in the car once they saw the place. Susan had provided me with a microphone in the shape of a pen. I placed it on the table next to a notepad I had brought along for appearance's sake.

An emaciated woman in a worn pink waitress uniform came and took my order of coffee. Mrs. Livingston ordered a breakfast of eggs and sausage with biscuits and gravy.

"Thanks for meeting me. I'm doing some investigative work at the bequest of Joan Wilcox, the sheriff in Burnet County. It seems her detectives came to a dead end in investigating the four similar murders, and therefore I'm here to see if you could shed any light on why your niece might have been murdered."

"The only person that I know of that might have murdered Delores was that damn worthless ex-husband of hers. He used to beat the hell out of her, until she got rescued over at that shelter. I forget the name of it."

"Mourning Doves?"

"That's right. They saved her life. Of course, working here in this dump and taking care of her demented mother, my sister, may not sound like living to you."

"I try not to judge other people's decisions about their lives unless it somehow interferes with my life. Is her mother completely gone, or still partially mentally intact?"

"She's in and out. I take care of her when Delores is—was, rather—at work. Don't know what I'll do now, with her gone."

Her food arrived, which looked like a runny pile of glop compared to the breakfast Mary Louise and I had made that morning. But to each their own.

"I've found a common thread between two of the victims, and wonder if Delores had ever had any psychiatric problems?"

Sarah chewed her breakfast for a moment, then nodded her head. "Yes. It was a while back. She went into a depression, could hardly get out of bed. Then one night, when her mother, my sister, was still lucid, she called me and said Delores had gone crazy, and to come right away. Well, I went over there, and she was absolutely raising hell and manic as she could be. I called 911 and the EMTs took her away. She ended up in Austin. They kept her for three months, and when she came back, she was calm as a cucumber. Said she had to take this little pill once a day for the rest of her life. And she did, as far as I know. Never had another episode."

"Do you remember where they took her? And the name of the medication she was taking?"

"No. Been too long."

"Would you mind looking through her things and see if you can find any records about either the institution or the medication?"

"I'll check and see. Can't promise anything, though."

"I understand. Here's my card. I'll take care of breakfast, and thanks for meeting me."

I dropped off two $20 bills at the counter next to where our waitress was standing.

"Well, thank you sir. Come back anytime," she said and smiled, exposing rows of brown and missing teeth. I felt that I should have left her more money.

Susan and Mary Louise had heard our conversation through the magic of the pen microphone transmitter, and we three concurred that there was something revelatory in the conversation.

"We've encountered medical history of a psychological breakdown of some sort in three of our four victims, followed by a hospitalization at a location in Austin that resulted in each taking a daily pill for the rest of their lives. I think that's important, Jim Bob," said Susan.

"I agree. Three out of four victims had psychiatric issues requiring hospitalization and long-term medication. If Freddie Simons's father confirms that his son had issues as well, we've found a common thread. I have no idea what it means, however. This could all be coincidental, since there are many, many people with mental health issues out there."

"Maybe," said Susan, "but I think we're beyond the statistical norms. There is something lurking beneath the surface that we can't see yet. But we are making headway. Good job, friend!" she said, and patted my shoulder from the back seat.

Freddie Simons's father met us at his home in Marble Falls. He lived just off the water of Lake Marble Falls, which was created by a dam in the Colorado River. The neighborhood was seasoned but the houses had been maintained, despite their proximity to the water, with fresh paint and well-kept yards. He was sitting on the front porch when we arrived, and he stood to greet us. He was taller than I but was very thin. He wore faded jeans, a plaid shirt, and an orange-and-white baseball cap with the Texas Longhorn emblem. His head was shaved over the ears and around his neck, and he sported a gray goatee.

"Fred Simons," he said, and extended his hand. "I'm the Senior, Freddie is—was—the Junior. That's what our friends called us, Senior and Junior."

I introduced him to Susan and Mary Louise as participants in the interviews I was conducting regarding the recent slayings, and again my role as an assistant to the sheriff.

"You know, I lost Freddie's mother to cancer a couple of years back. It was just Freddie and me. He was an only child. You folks are welcome to sit."

The women looked at the choices of seats on the porch and picked out ones that would not interfere with the line of sight between Fred Simons and myself.

"What can you tell me about your son?" I asked.

"He was a good boy. Never gave me a bit of trouble. I was worried about him when he started high school, because you know what kind of trouble kids get into with what people like to call their peer group. But not Freddie. He worked all through high school at the HEB, and I think that hard work and responsibility kept him on the straight and narrow. He bought his own car, paid his insurance, took care of his clothes. After his momma died, well, he was pretty much on his own."

"If you don't mind me asking, what is your occupation?"

"Postal worker, United States Post Office. Been doing that since I got back from my stint in the army after high school. They pay you a living wage and you would have to do something terrible to get fired. Plus, you get good health benefits and good retirement pay."

"Was Freddie following in your footsteps?"

"No. After high school he wanted to join up for the military, but he had a history of mental problems, and the army classified him as 4-F. So, the HEB offered him a position in managerial training, and he took it. You would not think so, maybe, but the grocery business offers good benefits and a good salary and for a kid like Freddie, and that was good enough for him."

"And how old was Freddie?"

"He had just turned twenty-two."

"And what kind of mental problems did he have?"

"He had bipolar disorder, with those mood swings. They were not very often, but when he had them, it was not pretty. We eventually got referred to a place in Austin. They put him on some medications that changed his life."

"Could I look at his prescription bottle, please?"

"I don't see why not. Freddie won't be needing them." He left the porch and went inside.

"Ask him about the hospitalization, Jim, and why he was at the Stop and Go," said Susan.

"Will do."

Fred Simons returned and handed me four pill bottles. "There was another, I think, but I didn't see it in his bathroom."

"He lived at home, with you?"

"Yes, sir. He was making decent money, but why pay rent when you can live at home for free? I work the day shift and Freddie usually had an evening shift, so we rarely saw each other."

"Do you have any idea what he was doing at the Stop and Go in Horseshoe Bay the night he was killed?"

Mr. Simons hung his head. "Yep. A girl."

"You mean, like a girlfriend?"

"Yes. He went to high school with her, and they had one of those teenage love things. I thought it would pass once they graduated, especially since she went off to UT in Austin for college. Freddie would be no match for those college boys. But there was something between them, and when she came home for breaks, she would call him, and it would start up again. She called him that night, and he headed over there after work. He was working his usual late-afternoon/early-evening shift at the time. He stopped at the Stop and Go for beer probably."

"And where was he meeting the girl? At her home?"

"Yes. She lives over in Horseshoe Bay. Daddy's a doctor, at the medical center, I think."

"Would you mind giving me her name?"

"Shannon. Shannon Wright."

"Well," I said as I stood, "thanks for the information. I hope it leads to the arrest and conviction of whoever is killing these people."

"No clues so far?"

"No, sorry to say. Other than the fact that all four victims seemed to have had mental health issues."

"You might talk to Shannon. She was there for a stint, just like Freddie."

"You mean in the hospital?"

"Yep. Blue Lake in Austin."

# CHAPTER 12

# MEDICATION RESEARCH

**A**ll that interviewing had made me hungry, so we stopped at the Bluebonnet Café for lunch on the way home. Country fried steak with cream gravy stimulated my brain cells for a short time. Unfortunately, it also stimulated my sleep cells, so I had to get real smart quickly after lunch, otherwise I would be in nap mode.

What did I really know at that time, after reviewing the sheriff's files and interviewing four family members of the victims? All four had a history of mental illness. Two had been admitted to a mental health facility in Austin called Blue Lake. Hubert Brown had a history of having had electroshock therapy, and had only one pill bottle, of which he took one capsule daily, and had done ever since his hospitalization. Delores White also had only one pill bottle and took one pill daily.

Noni Berry and Freddie Simons had multiple pill bottles, Noni with six and Freddie with four, but there could have been more in Freddie's case. Noni had been taught to select her pills based on her anticipated mood swings and other factors I did not understand. Since Freddie had multiple pill bottles, I had to assume he had similar instructions, but there was no proof of that from his father.

The two young people, Noni and Freddie, had significant mental health problems and had been hospitalized at Blue Lake Hospital in Austin, and Noni's mother and Freddie's father had called the institution by name. Both had multiple pill bottles and were "dosing" based on mood swings. The two older folks, Hubert and Delores, had been hospitalized, but neither knew the name of the institution. Both were taking only one pill per day. Was that due to an age difference between the victims? Or a different treatment regimen?

I needed to follow up with Hubert Brown's ex, Lizzie Brown, and see if she had found records of his hospitalization. I needed the same information from Delores White's aunt, Sarah Livingston, as well as her pill bottle.

I also realized that I was significantly deficient in my knowledge of modern psychiatric terminology and treatment. Medications to treat the mentally ill were few and far between back when I was in medical school.

I went to my desk and opened the computer, typed "mental health issues" into the search engine, and was presented with reams of websites from psychiatric hospitals, mental health clinics, and pharmaceutical companies. There were so many options, I decided I needed a nap before I could sort all the information available. Mary Louise had opted for an immediate nap after lunch at Bluebonnet, so I crept into the bedroom and quickly joined her in dreamland.

Refreshed and coffee in hand, I started with several physician-oriented websites that discussed the most common mental illness diagnoses. They were major depressive disorder, generalized anxiety disorder, bipolar disorder, dementia, attention deficit hyperactivity disorder (ADHD), schizoaffective disorder, obsessive-compulsive disorder (OCD), and post-traumatic stress disorder (PTSD).

Major depressive disorder was described as being characterized by a persistently depressed mood with loss of interest in all activities, causing significant impairment in daily life. Depression could be a stand-alone diagnosis or could be combined with manic symptoms to create bipolar disorder.

The sites described bipolar disorder as including manic episodes that produced high energy, reduced need for sleep, and loss of touch with reality. The accompanying depressive episodes could include low energy, low motivation, and loss of interest in daily activities. The mood episodes lasted days to weeks or even months at a time and were sometimes associated with suicidal thoughts.

Looking at the other common mental health disorders, generalized anxiety disorder didn't seem to be a part of the four victims' symptomology, at least according to the relatives I spoke to. Neither did dementia, ADHD, OCD, or PTSD. My recollection from med school was that schizophrenia, now schizoaffective disorder, was the same as bipolar disorder, but when I researched the differences, I found that the hallmark symptoms of schizophrenia included hallucinations and delusions, which was not described as a part of bipolar disorder. That's a diagnosis of mania alternating with depression but without the hallucinatory component.

Looking at the big picture of mental illness in the four victims, based on family interviews and literature research, bipolar disorder seemed to be the most likely diagnosis in each case. That would explain the "one pill daily cure" of Hubert Brown and Delores White. The two younger victims, however, were taking multiple pills based on their mood swings, or perhaps other factors I was not aware of. Did that mean that they both had other diagnoses for which they were taking other medications? I had not a clue. I would need to get my hands on the medical records from all victims, if possible. Still, none of my research pointed to a "smoking gun" that would explain why or how the four victims were tied together in some fashion resulting in their traumatic demise.

I did some further research on bipolar disorder and unfortunately found that, on occasion, three of the other diagnoses that made up the most common mental health disorders—generalized anxiety disorder, ADD, and OCD—were related to bipolar disorder. Perhaps that was a clue as to why Freddie and Noni were on multiple medications. It was bad enough to have a child with one mental health disorder, but to have four different diagnoses at the same time in the same person would be a nightmare for parent and child. I would need to research the medications for treatment for these various disorders and explore the prescription bottles I had from Hubert Brown, Noni, and Freddie.

I left messages with Lizzie Brown and Sarah Livingston, reminding Lizzie to look through Hubert's files to see where he was hospitalized and reminding Sarah to see if she had found the information on Delores's hospitalization as well as her one medication bottle.

I reviewed the literature on medications for the treatment of bipolar disorder. Just reading about the drugs and their side effects was startling and overwhelming.

Mood stabilizers could be used to control the manic episodes. There were many available, including Lithium, Depakote, Tegretol, and Lamictal. Antipsychotics were prescribed to combat the depression portion of the disorder, and included Zyprexa, Risperdal, Seroquel, Abilify, Geodon, and Saphris. Sometimes, however, an antidepressant triggered a manic episode, and so additional medications were indicated, such as Symbyax, which combined the antidepressant fluoxetine and the antipsychotic olanzapine, which worked as an antidepressant and mood stabilizer. Also, anti-anxiety meds were sometimes needed for sleep because of all the other drugs that were necessary, so benzodiazepines were often used on a short-term basis. And psychotherapy was often an integral part of bipolar treatment. God help you, though, if you had alcohol and/or drug abuse problems. Then the medications could kill you. Bipolar disorder was a horrible and miserable affliction for all concerned.

I set Noni's pill bottles next to Freddie's pill bottles on my desk. All four of Freddie's meds matched Noni's meds. Whether his dad would be able to come up with more prescription drugs or not probably didn't matter. I reviewed my notes from the online search, and three of the meds of each patient were listed in the common drugs used to treat bipolar disorder. Each was on Depakote, a mood stabilizer, Risperdal, an antidepressant and antipsychotic, and Symbyax, a combined antidepressant and mood stabilizer used to reduce the chance of a manic episode being triggered by the antidepressant. For reasons that were not apparent to me, Noni was also on two drugs considered to be antipsychotics and antidepressants, Seroquel and Saphris. Perhaps she had a worse or slightly different form of the disorder than Freddie and needed additional medication. And according to her mother, Noni had the ability to appropriately control the meds she took to get through any given day. That would require a great deal of trust on the part of her parents and physicians.

Each of the victims had a prescription for a drug that was not listed in any of the material I'd reviewed. It was named on the prescription bottle as Equiliminbital. I looked up that medication and found no references to it in the medical literature. I thought that maybe it could be an experimental drug of some sort, and that Noni and Freddie were part of a study of bipolar disorder.

Double-blind studies are research studies where one set of patients gets the testing drug, and the other set gets a placebo. These were not uncommon in the pharmaceutical field. And I assumed that if Blue Lake Psychiatric was a legitimate treatment facility, they could be performing clinical trials for a pharmaceutical company, or even the government.

I had been using my phone as well as my computer to research these mental disorders, so when I took a break, I noticed there were a couple of missed messages on my cell phone. The first was from Lizzie Brown, who again thanked me for caring about Hubert Brown, her ex-husband, and told me that she had found the name of the hospital he had been admitted to. It was called Blue Lake in the Austin area. Also, she had discovered a handwritten prescription from his doctor for Hubert's daily medication, and while neither she nor I had been able to read the name on the pill bottle, the written script clearly read Equiliminbital.

Sarah Livingston also had called and confirmed that Blue Lake was where her niece had been admitted. She spelled out the name of the drug Delores White was taking daily because she couldn't pronounce it. It was Equiliminbital as well, same as Hubert Brown.

There were four randomly murdered people, all on the same drug for bipolar disorder, all having been admitted and treated at the same hospital. The youngest, Noni, was on six different medications. The other youngster, Freddie, was on four medications. The two middle-aged patients were on one medication, the same as the two young people who were also on other medications.

At that point, I wondered what the hell any of this meant. Were the murder victims randomly chosen, or was there another connection? My next move would be to research Blue Lake online and find out what sort of facility it was. Then, I probably would have to work my way into Blue Lake and find out what I could in person. I knew doctors, and I knew hospitals and hospital administrators, and I would have to be prepared to be stonewalled unless I had plenty of power and influence on my side, such as the patients' families and an element of law enforcement. I hoped that Sheriff Joan Wilcox and ASAC Susan Beeson would come to my rescue, because these cases to me felt like trouble brewing and involved maybe something deeper than what on the surface appeared to be murders by a random serial killer.

# CHAPTER 13

# DAY JOB

The shrill screeching of the alarm woke me Monday morning. I showered and shaved and left my family in the bed, grabbed a to-go cup of coffee, and headed to the hospital. It was time for me to remove the metaphorical Sherlock Holmes deerstalker hat, put on an actual surgical cap and hood, and ply my trade as an orthopedic surgeon.

Belinda met me at 6 a.m. on the hospital floor. There were a couple of folks left from Wednesday surgery who had not gone to rehab or left for home. There were also two new patients she had admitted over the weekend who were scheduled for surgery that day. One was an older fellow who had fallen out of bed at the nursing home and broken his hip. He carried a diagnosis of Alzheimer's disease and appeared to be disoriented and confused. He was restrained with cloth ties around his wrists and ankles. He had been brought in by the EMTs from his place of residence; no family had appeared since he had been admitted.

The other patient was a college student, home for the weekend, who had flirted with new moves on his skateboard which had ended in a disastrous crash along a stretch of seawall built to protect houses on Horseshoe Bay from rising water. He would have drowned, had his friends not jumped into the lake and pulled him to shore, broken leg and all. He was an unhappy camper named Matt Solis. His mother was at his bedside.

"Morning, I'm Dr. Brady."

"Beverly Solis," she said, and extended a hand. "Can you patch the boy up, Doc?"

"Yes, although when his knee encountered the concrete seawall, he shattered the kneecap as well as his tibia and femur. I can fix the two leg bones, but the kneecap is in so many pieces I'll probably have to remove it and sew the quadriceps muscle to the lower patellar tendon. It won't be as efficient a mechanism as the good Lord made, but it'll be adequate, outside of athletics. His skateboard days are probably done."

The boy was sobbing at that point.

"Sorry, son, but you need to know the prognosis from the start. I'll do the best I can, but without a kneecap, you just won't have the leg strength you had before. What's your major?"

"Accounting," he said, sniffling.

"Perfect."

We had six other cases to do that day: two hip replacements, three knee replacements, and a hip arthroscopy for a torn labrum. I had done a few of the latter procedures, and so far the patients had enjoyed excellent results. The trick was to have the surgery done prior to the patient developing arthritis in the hip joint. Repairing a torn labrum in the presence of hip arthritis was an exercise in futility.

Eight cases were two more than my normal, so the day ran longer than I liked. The six elective procedures were routine. The gentleman from the nursing home with the fractured hip, Ben Harper, gave me fits. X-rays showed his fracture extended down into the shaft of the femur and would require a custom plate to capture all the pieces. We had to call the manufacturer's rep, who had to drive over from Austin with the appropriate hardware, so that delayed the start of his surgery. As to young Matt Solis's injury, he had done a number on the bones above and below the knee joint. The patella had to be removed, as I had told them prior to surgery. The tibia required a side plate with a flange across the bone below the knee joint. The femur fracture had required a side plate as well, with multiple screws to capture the smaller pieces. We used two operating rooms, but even with the efficient routine Belinda and I had developed, we walked out of surgery at 7 p.m., bone tired.

By the time I talked to the families, checked on the post-op patients, and dictated the op reports, I wandered over to my office at 8:30 p.m. Maya had gone home and had left me a few notes. There was nothing urgent on my desk, so I took the elevator down the two flights and boarded my truck for home.

I saw a flash as I backed up, and the small figure I had seen two other times was around my truck as if in perpetual motion. He tried to jump onto the hood, but I gunned the accelerator and made it to the open space outside the garage, and he rolled off. Then he came around the rear of the vehicle and tried to open the front passenger door. I was too tired to mess with it all, so I pulled my .357 Smith and Wesson Magnum revolver out of the glove box, lowered the driver window, and fired two shots into the air. After that, the assailant disappeared.

By the time I got home, I was almost asleep. Mary Louise had made toasted cheese sandwiches and soup. I ate numbly, showered, and crawled into bed. The clock read 9:58 p.m. I was going to tell her about the little man who attacked the car but thought better of it.

Five o'clock a.m. came early but I got up and started another day. Rounds with Belinda went smoothly, and there were no overnight problems for the patients. Beverly Solis was at her son's bedside in a chair that fooled patients' visitors into thinking it was a recliner until they woke up with interminable lumbar spine pain.

"You slept here?" I asked.

"Yes. What we do for our kids. You said the surgery went all right, about what you expected?"

"Yes, but it really was a bad injury. He's going to be disabled for a while. He'll need a walker, crutches, a wheelchair, maybe even a hospital bed at home. Where does he go to school?"

"Southwestern in Georgetown."

"Can they make arrangements for him for a few months and allow him to attend virtually?"

"I'll find out today. I sure would hate to see him lose the semester."

"If you need letters, or emails, or a stern nurse to yell at a college dean, let Belinda know."

She laughed. "Thanks much."

I had a bite to eat in the doctor's lounge, then started clinic a little past 7 a.m. It was a busy day there as well, and we had to take turns having lunch to get everyone seen by 5 p.m. We three limped up to the office, cleared our respective desks, and went home.

I called Dr. Jerry Reed on the way home. He was still doing an autopsy, so I was not the only doctor who worked long hours. I muttered that I should quit feeling sorry for myself and be glad I had a successful practice.

"Jerry, I have a question."

"I'm not surprised at that. What is it?"

"Regarding these four cases of murder by bludgeoning, I've been doing a little investigating on the side, and after talking to relatives of each, I've discovered that each had a diagnosis of bipolar disorder and were on medications for the problem. My question is, can you test blood for the drugs they were prescribed?"

"Well, aren't you the clever one?"

"What do you mean? I was asked by Sheriff Joan Wilcox to look through the files and see if I saw anything the detectives might have missed, or any common threads linking the four victims."

"Yes, I know that. You told me all about it. I mentioned the word 'clever' because I'm curious how you picked up that mental health link?"

"Well, I interviewed Hubert Brown's ex-wife, and it came up in conversation that he was on one drug for bipolar, and then I asked subsequent family members I interviewed about their particular loved one and discovered the common thread."

"I'm ahead of you."

"What do you mean?"

"I took blood from all the victims and ran tests for toxins and medications as usual. I discovered they all were on psychotropics of some kind, some on more than others."

"And did you find the single medication that they were all on?"

"No. I found common links, like Risperdal, Depakote, Symbyax, common drugs used to treat bipolar disorder. However, I didn't find evidence that there was one drug each of the patients was taking in common."

"Equiliminbital. That's the drug. Each victim had a prescription bottle for it."

"Never heard of it, so I could not test for it."

"Can you check it out in a blood screening process?"

"Not if we've never heard of it. I was able to pick up the common psych drugs easily, but that drug, I don't know about it. Could be experimental, part of a study of some sort."

"I thought the same thing. Anyway, maybe we can work together on it. I was able to glean the name of the hospital in Austin where all four victims had been treated. It's called Blue Lake."

"Me, do pharmacological sleuthing with you? I am the Chief of Pathology, and the County Coroner, and what are you? An orthopedic surgeon acting like he is a part-time Sherlock Holmes?"

"I have the files, I have the name of the hospital, I have the investigative authority of the sheriff of Burnet County, and the ASAC of the Austin FBI, Susan Beeson, is our best friend and has my back."

"There is that . . ."

Tip acted as though I had been gone on sabbatical for months. Mary Louise greeted me with open arms. I felt like I had not seen her in days, Monday and Tuesday having been what they were.

"I thought you would be whipped again, so I made meat loaf, one of your favorites, along with scalloped potatoes and a Caesar salad. How about a drink, tired and worn-out husband?"

"That would be great."

She handed me a single-malt Balvenie scotch with one ice cube. We toasted each other and caught up on our activities for the past two days. She put out the food and we helped ourselves in buffet fashion.

"Susan called me this morning and wondered if you had made any discoveries since our sojourn Sunday to visit family members of the deceased. I told her that I doubted it, since you were at the hospital until after 8 p.m. yesterday and were just now coming home from a long clinic day."

"I did manage to talk to Jerry Reed on the way home. He had already discovered that all four victims had been on psychotropic drugs of one type or another. He was familiar with all the medications except one and had already discovered, via the drugs he found in their respective systems, that most likely the deceased each had bipolar disorder. Looking through the files that Joan Wilcox gave me, there was no mention of mental health problems in any of the murder victims. That isn't a big surprise, since each of them reportedly had their conditions well-managed via medication.

"Jerry and I did find one drug common to each patient, but he hadn't heard of it before, and therefore he couldn't test for it, and I could find nothing about the drug on the internet."

"What was the name of the drug?"

"Equiliminbital."

"You can rest assured I've never heard of it either, not that I'm any sort of expert in the field."

"At some point, I'll have to have a conversation with Susan about how to proceed. This place in Austin called Blue Lake will have to be approached carefully. They could be sitting on a powder keg of information, and with four murdered patients of theirs, all on the same bipolar disorder drug, there could be a significant liability issue."

"Not to represent their interests, but it's possible that this could be a coincidence, that Blue Lake is totally innocent of any wrongdoing, and these serial killings are totally unrelated to their patients and their respective medications."

"And the moon could fall out of the sky tomorrow, Mary Louise."

"I'm just saying, Jim Bob, if you continue to be involved in these murders, that if you approach Blue Lake with the attitude that their institution is somehow at fault, you'll get nowhere. They will be defensive from the start if you go in there with an accusatory attitude. You must approach the administration and the doctors with an open mind, and portray sympathy, and act like you, as a physician and surgeon, are on their side, and are trying to help them, not embarrass them. That will get you a lot further than riding in there on your white horse and acting like you're there to slay the dragon. I know how you can be."

"Mary Louise, I'll do my best to be professional, if allowed by the powers that be to continue what I have started. But it defies logic to think there is not something going on at that hospital. Four murdered patients, and all on the same drug for bipolar disorder. Something is rotten in Denmark. I am sure of it."

"There may be, Jim Bob, but you can catch more flies with honey than with vinegar, which is an adage that implies you can win people to your side more easily by gentle persuasion and flattery than by hostile confrontation."

I stared at her for an anxious moment, then took a deep breath. "You are so right, Mary Louise. I'll have to work on that technique."

"I'll clean up while you shower," she said, as she leaned over and kissed me. The kiss lingered a little longer than necessary.

"If you need a massage, let me know," she whispered.

"I would never turn down one of your massages, regardless of how tired I might be."

I entered the primary bedroom, stripped down, got into the shower, and turned the water on to hot. I cleaned myself of the day's activities, got out and dried off, and put on a pair of boxer shorts. I exited the bathroom to find my bride lying on the bed, propped on one elbow, stark naked, with a bottle of body lotion in hand.

"You won't need those boxers, fella," she said.

## CHAPTER 14

# THE BADGE

I would never have said this in my younger days, but I was thrilled that two of our six cases for Wednesday had to be rescheduled. That left Belinda and me two hip and two knee replacements to do. Compared to the schedule we had lately been burdened with, a four-case schedule was like a day off.

We made rounds as usual at 6 a.m., started surgery at 7 and were done by 3 p.m. I was in a great mood, partially due to the schedule reduction for the day, and partly due to the affections of Mary Louise Brady. I cheerily cleaned off my desk, made the requisite phone calls, and signed the required documents.

I made a list of things to do involving the alleged serial killer matters, the first being to speak to both Joan Wilcox and Susan Beeson regarding my status in the cases. I called Sheriff Wilcox's office first.

"Sheriff's office, Deputy Baldwin speaking."

"Hey, Sharon, this is Dr. Brady. How are you this fine day?"

"Oh, Dr. Brady, I'm just fine, sir," she replied warmly. "Are you coming by today?"

"Sorry, but no. I just need to speak to her briefly."

"Oh, I am sorry to hear that. You're always welcome in our offices."

"I appreciate that, Sharon. Is she in?"

"I believe so, Dr. Brady. Let me put you through."

I waited for a moment, heard clicks in the background, then "And how is my newest detective?"

"I'm good, Joan. I have a few things to discuss with you," I said, and went through the combined findings of Jerry Reed and myself.

"I am amazed at the progress you've made. And all this information came from the family members, including the prescription bottles?"

"Yes, ma'am, and your files, of course."

"To summarize, we have four patients from Blue Lake, some sort of psychiatric facility in Austin, all with bipolar disorder, all on the same medication, bludgeoned to death behind four different grocery stores. Does that sum it up?"

"Exactly."

"What do you want to do next?"

"Go to Blue Lake, find out what I can about the patients and the facility. I'll need credentials of some sort, more than likely. What would you suggest?"

"Well, I can deputize you and give you a badge. We've used special investigators in the past, and there's no reason why we cannot do that again. Do you feel the need to be accompanied by one of my official detectives, perhaps one of the two original investigators?"

"I would prefer not. There could be some animosity between the two investigators and me, and I would not want that to distract my interviews there. Also, I think Dr. Jerry Reed, the coroner, wants to get involved, so he and I could go together. No badge necessary for Dr. Reed, though."

"Fine. When would you be going up there?"

"I don't know. Maya will try and make an appointment, but I need an 'in' of some sort. Can I let you know?"

"Sure. Meanwhile, let me have someone deliver that badge to you."

"That would be terrific. I may or may not be here, though."

"Not a problem. I'll get it over there today. And thanks again."

Next, I called Susan Beeson and apprised her of the situation as well. "And Joan offered to give you a shield? I am shocked. At least I won't have to come up with a ridiculous excuse to try and give you an FBI badge."

"You can do that?"

She paused for a moment. "Don't even go there, Jim Bob Brady. The director would have MY badge if I even thought about that. When are you going to Blue Lake?"

"I don't know yet. I thought I had to find a reason to talk to the staff, but with a badge and special investigator status, I guess I could just waltz in unannounced and tell them I'm investigating the murder of four of their former patients."

"Catch them off guard. Good idea. I can provide you with a letter from the ASAC—that would be me—asking the facility administrator to provide you with every courtesy. That usually is impressive. You could stop by here and pick it up once you're in Austin."

"Wow. A badge from the sheriff and an 'every courtesy' letter from the FBI. That's sort of a license to steal, for a guy like me."

"Don't remind me, old friend. Make me proud."

I called Jerry Reed next and asked him if he would be available to take a trip to Austin on Friday and interview the staff at Blue Lake. He said he would gladly clear his schedule. I opened my office door and motioned Maya Stern to enter.

"Okay, I'm cleared to make a trip to Blue Lake in Austin. Sheriff Wilcox is delivering a badge today, so please secure it. I also will have a letter from the FBI entailing my legitimacy to be asking questions, which I'll pick up once in Austin, which I'm thinking will be Friday. Is my schedule clear that day?"

"Yes, sir, as of now. If any emergencies arise today or tomorrow, I'll get one of your associates to take care of the problems."

"Please make sure you avail them of Belinda's skills. She can handle most orthopedic issues."

"Yes sir, will do."

"I want to thank you for your diligence in putting those interviews together. So much information about those murders has been gained by your persistence. You almost broke the case open, so not only do I thank you, but law enforcement does as well."

She reddened. "Thank you, Dr. Brady. Excuse me, but I need to get my phone."

I leaned back in my office chair and studied the ceiling for a moment. Maya returned and told me to call my wife, that there was an emergency.

"What's going on?" I asked Mary Louise.

"It's Bob Jackson. He went on another bender and lost control. Annie had to call 911 again."

"Didn't he just finish detox here? And was he not supposed to go to a drug and alcohol rehab center immediately after discharge?"

"Yes, but he told Annie he felt great, and that he was well and cured, never to drink again. And that he didn't need more rehab."

"He never got rehab. He was detoxed only. That was only a partial treatment for his problem."

"I know that, and you know that, and Annie knows that. Bob doesn't know that, or at least he didn't believe it."

"Are the EMTs bringing him back here for another detox?"

"No. His insurance wouldn't approve it, since he didn't complete their criteria for readmission, which is mainly to complete the rehab program."

"So where is he going?"

"A drug and alcohol hospital in Austin. Jim Bob, Annie said she thought it was called Blue Lake."

CHAPTER 15

# BLUE LAKE

I had canceled my standing golf game for Friday to make the trek to Austin to evaluate Blue Lake Psychiatric Hospital. I looked up the institution online and found it was off Steiner Road near Lake Travis, described to be in an idyllic setting in a wooded area. The hospital catered to those with mental health issues, and it included a significant drug and alcohol treatment center as part of the campus. There was a long list of board-certified psychiatrists in residence there, along with psychologists with PhD degrees and social workers with MSW degrees who specialized in counseling the addicted. The hospital appeared to be, at least on the internet, a top-ranked facility with high approval ratings from all the right organizations and had an accreditation by the joint commission. On the surface, and on paper, the facility appeared to be one of the best. I knew in my heart that evil lurked there somewhere, but I had no evidence whatsoever to prove that.

I was armed with my Burnet County deputy sheriff badge, which had been delivered in person by none other than Deputy Sharon Baldwin. I had picked up my "credentials" from Susan Beeson at the FBI office on Research Boulevard off Highway 183 on the way into town prior to visiting Blue Lake. The FBI offices were way out of the way, so I had to waste twenty minutes or so doubling back toward Lake Travis to get to the hospital.

"Do you know where you're going, Brady?" asked Dr. Jerry Reed, my passenger, co-conspirator, and back seat driver. I had picked him up in the doctor's parking garage before departing east toward the Big City.

"Of course not, but the navigation system seems to be taking us in the right direction."

I had dressed in nice slacks, crocodile boots, and a sports jacket. I asked Jerry to do the same, but he was in wrinkled jeans, athletic shoes, and a tee shirt. At least he had on a jacket, which was wrinkled to match his jeans.

"Go over your plan with me again. You're going to show up unannounced at Blue Lake, demand to speak to whoever is in charge, then expect them to open their medical records on the four deceased victims without a complaint?"

"Jerry, I have a badge, I have a credentials letter from ASAC Beeson at the FBI, and I have Release of Information forms signed by the patients' families."

That was a stroke of genius on the part of Maya and Belinda. They dealt with the day-to-day workings of a doctor's office much more than I, so when they suggested taking along Release of Information forms, they basically said that I would get nowhere without them. They had been nice enough to call Lizzie Brown, Sarah Livingston, Trish Berry, and Fred Simons and asked each to come into the office to sign the forms that permitted me to review and evaluate and make copies of their family members' medical records. On the off chance I would need to speak to someone in charge of Bob Jackson's treatment, Annie had signed a Release of Information form as well.

We pulled up into a valet parking area in front of Blue Lake, a four-story facility of brown brick. My first thought was why brown? The Texas Hill Country is full of limestone in all sorts of shades of tan, white, and cream; how much better the exterior of the facility would have looked with a limestone facade.

"Just visiting, sir?" asked the valet parker.

"Yes, at least I hope so," I said, smiling.

He just gave a curt nod, which caused me to reflect on how often we joke about mental health thoughtlessly. Plus, he'd probably heard that one about a hundred times before.

He gave me a ticket stub. I gathered up the documents I had brought, put them in my briefcase, and Jerry and I went through the automatic sliding front door. The lobby was decorated in a modern motif, with a lot of sleek black furniture and glass tables. To me, it was cold and off-putting, but I imagined there had been many studies about what interior design would be best suited for this particular purpose.

There was a circular desk in the center of the room, where two women with nursing uniforms sat. Both had white hair and wore glasses, and they were probably volunteers.

"May I help you?" asked the woman whose name plate read Mildred Bland.

"Yes," I said. "I need to speak to whoever is in charge please."

She looked at her coworker, whose name plate read Lila Olsen. They conferred out of hearing range for a moment, then Mildred asked, "Which department? Alcohol rehab? Drug rehab? Pharmacology? Psychiatry? Psychology? Family counseling? Hospital administration?"

I looked at Jerry, and he shrugged. "I think hospital administration would be appropriate for starters."

"That would be Dr. Seth McIntyre. And may I ask what your business with him is?"

"We're here about four of your patients who've been murdered out in the Hill Country."

That comment brought dropped jaws, then activity from both women. Phone calls were made immediately, and Dr. McIntyre was located. "He'll be right here. Please have a seat and make yourself comfortable," said Mildred.

We found a quiet spot off to the side of the entry overlooking a forest, the "idyllic" setting from the internet description, I surmised. We were the only people in the lobby other than the two greeters at the entry desk.

"It's going well so far," I said to Jerry.

"Nothing has happened, Brady. We're sitting here waiting on the hospital administrator and have no idea if he has any knowledge of the fate of the four former patients or not."

"We will soon find out. I bet that's him coming off the elevator."

Dr. McIntyre headed first to the desk, then veered our way after a hand gesture from Mildred.

"Seth McIntyre," he said, extending his hand to Jerry, then me.

"I'm Dr. Jim Brady, orthopedic surgeon at Hill Country Medical Center, and this is my colleague Dr. Jerry Reed, Burnet County coroner and chief of pathology at HCMC. Thank you for seeing us."

"Mildred said something about four of our patients having been murdered. What was she talking about?"

"Perhaps we could go somewhere and speak privately," I said.

"Of course. We can go up to the conference room on the fourth floor. I've taken the liberty of notifying Dr. William Watson, head of psychiatry, about your visit. He can meet us in the conference room as well." We stood and walked to the elevator. Dr. McIntyre was a couple of inches shorter than me, had short brown hair, wore glasses, and had on a blue suit with a yellow tie.

"Have either of you been here before?"

Jerry and I both shook our heads.

"Blue Lake was built about twenty years ago. It was a dream of Dr. Watson's to build a state-of-the-art facility to handle the needs of all mental health patients, including an alcohol and drug rehabilitation program. The first floor houses a cafeteria, a small shop for sundries, and an area for patients to meet with their loved ones in a more normal setting than on the hospital floor. The second floor is reserved for the housing and treatment of our alcohol- and drug-addicted patients, and includes private rooms, physical therapy, occupational therapy, and a small movie theater. The third floor houses the more severely ill patients, some of whom are here for a short period of time and then return to society, and some who live here permanently because their needs cannot be met in the outside world. The top floor is reserved for administration and physicians' offices. That's also the location of our conference room."

The conference room was located adjacent to the entry lobby on the fourth floor. We walked in and found coffee, sodas, water, pastries, and finger sandwiches. The mahogany table was surrounded by twelve chairs.

"Please help yourselves, gentlemen," said Dr. McIntyre.

"With this spread, it seems you knew we were coming," Jeff replied.

"We always keep food and beverages on hand. In a facility such as this, with our patient population, events can happen on the spur of the moment, necessitating consultation with doctors and family members on an emergency basis. We've found that food and drink mitigate a person's anxiety and make for better conversation and decision-making, so our kitchen staff always has food prepared."

"I think I'd like to work here," I said. "I'm always worried about getting food and being hydrated. This concept would eliminate those issues, especially when I'm in the operating room."

McIntyre laughed, then excused himself from the room.

"He seems normal to me, Brady. I was expecting a Gene Wilder character from *Young Frankenstein*."

"So was I. My only exposure to a mental health facility was the psych ward at the city-county hospital where I went to medical school. I've never been in a private psychiatric facility, and I had a lot of pre-conceived notions about what it would be like. I was thinking more of a *One Flew Over the Cuckoo's Nest* sort of environment."

"That's what the basement is for," Jerry responded.

"What basement?" I asked. Before Jerry could retort with an inane response, Dr. McIntyre returned with another gentleman.

"Dr. Watson," he said, and shook our hands. "We heard some distressing news from one of the volunteers on level one. Can you give us a summary of what is going on, please?"

Dr. Watson was wearing a blue suit as well, and a red tie. His hair was gray, and he wore tortoise-shell glasses.

"I gave Dr. McIntyre our credentials," I said, and handed them our business cards. "I have a penchant for investigating mysteries, sometimes involving murder, and I have friends in law enforcement who appreciate that ability. In the matter of these murder cases, I was contacted by Sheriff Joan Wilcox of Burnet County and asked to participate in the investigation of what has turned out to be the murders of four citizens who lived in our area. Our area includes the string of towns that surround the Highland Lakes area in

Burnet and Llano counties, including Burnet, Marble Falls, Granite Falls, Horseshoe Bay, Llano, and Kingsland. She's appointed me a special investigator in this matter and provided me with the badge of a deputy sheriff of Burnet County.

"I'll also tell you that Susan Beeson, ASAC of the Austin FBI, has approved my presence in reviewing these cases, and I have a letter from her as well, authorizing my investigation. I'm happy to show you those credentials, and I have copies of the paperwork in my briefcase."

"We'll need copies of your credentials for our attorneys. I'm sure you understand," said Dr. McIntyre.

"Not a problem," I said, and opened the briefcase and gave him the originals to copy.

"I also have Release of Information forms for the four murder victims from their families, and you probably will need copies of those as well."

McIntyre took the original documents, went to the door, and called out for a staff member to make copies.

"Back to the heart of the matter. These murders started a little over three months ago. The first was Hubert Brown, fifty-six years old, and an x-ray technologist at HCMC. He was found behind a convenience store, having stopped there for snacks on his way to work. He was bludgeoned with a weapon resembling a hatchet or short axe. His ex-wife gave me the history that he had bipolar disorder and was hospitalized here some years ago for a period of three months, then returned home apparently cured, but had to take one pill daily to maintain his stability.

"The second victim was Delores White, a short-order cook, found behind a different convenience store that she had stopped at on her way home. She was killed in the same manner as the first victim. She had been hospitalized here at Blue Lake, according to her aunt, and was also taking the same medication as Mr. Brown.

"Then came Noni Berry, eighteen years old, killed and stuffed in the trunk of her boyfriend's car while he went into a different but larger grocery store to buy snacks. She was on six different medications, but one was the same medication the first two victims were taking.

"Last was Freddie Simons, twenty-two years old, killed in the same fashion and found in the refuse area of yet another grocery store. He was on four medications, but again, one that was common to the other three victims.

"I brought along the pill bottles from Hubert Brown, Noni Berry, and Freddie Simons. I don't have the pill bottle for Delores White but have a written spelling of the medication she was taking from her aunt, confirming all four were on the same drug.

"The drug that's common to all four patients is called Equiliminbital. I admit I don't know if that's a brand name or a generic name. I would like Dr. Reed to speak about that."

"Being a pathologist, and the coroner, I was tasked with the autopsies on these four individuals. As a matter of course, I ran a tox screen and checked blood levels for drugs, all kinds of drugs, not just the illicit ones. I found blood evidence in the two youngest people, Noni and Freddie, of drugs used to treat bipolar disorder—Risperdal, Depakote, and Symbyax. They each had, however, an unidentifiable drug, as did the two older victims, Hubert and Delores. I assume that the drug all four possessed in their blood at the time of death was this drug Equiliminbital, since each had a prescription bottle for that medication. I know nothing of this drug and was unable to discover any information about it from the literature or the internet. I suggested to Dr. Brady here that it might be experimental, and that maybe these four victims were involved in some sort of study at your institution."

"Why would you assume we had prescribed this medication? Because looking at the prescription bottles, there is no mention of Blue Lake on any of the bottles. It looks like two were filled at a pharmacy in Marble Falls, and two at a pharmacy in Horseshoe Bay," Dr. Watson commented.

"Well, that would have been an incorrect assumption on my part," I responded. "We have verbal confirmation from all four families that each victim had been treated at Blue Lake."

"And that may be so. We have staff locating the medical records of these individuals as we speak to confirm they were indeed patients here. But I must tell you, the name of the prescribing doctor on each of these bottles is not known to me or Dr. McIntyre. He is not a member of our staff. He is most likely a local physician involved in prescribing medications to the patients after discharge."

"But how can that be? A patient comes here for treatment, you provide the care and medication, and then after discharge the medications must be refilled."

"We provide the medications while a patient is here," said Dr. Watson, "and upon discharge, we also provide each patient with a thirty-day supply of medication. We liaise with physicians in the local communities to refill medications. Ours is a busy hospital and we are engaged in all sorts of research and treatment programs. We are not a medication refill source quite simply because we don't have the time. If a patient stops responding to the medications once they've left the hospital, the families return their loved ones to Blue Lake and a new regimen of medication is tried during a brief hospitalization. But again, the process would be repeated for the new medication. The local doctor refills the medication we've provided for the patient."

# CHAPTER 16

# HOSPITAL RECORDS

I felt the familiar facial burn of embarrassment because I had made a critical mistake in assuming each of the prescription drug vials I so proudly brought to Blue Lake had been filled or refilled by one of their very own physicians. I just did not pay close enough attention to the label. Had I inspected each more closely, it would have been apparent that the words Blue Lake were nowhere on the prescription. As for the prescribing doctor's name, I paid no attention whatsoever to that because I assumed it would be one of the in-residence physicians at Blue Lake and whose name I would not recognize anyway. I had played my hand poorly.

A silence had fallen over the conference room, broken by the entry of a young woman carrying a stack of files.

"Oh, thank you, Lisa," said Dr. Watson as she handed him what I assumed were the medical records of the four patients in question. He picked the top file and opened it.

"Hubert Brown was admitted here seventeen years ago with a diagnosis of acute mania as the alternating phase of bipolar disorder. He had been on several medications which were intermittently effective. According to the notes, he was wild and uncontrollable, and required immediate IV sedation.

He underwent electroconvulsive therapy, which improved his condition significantly. At the time, several medications were tried to control his mood swings, but the only one that consistently worked alone, without the aid of additional medications, was Equiliminbital."

"So, you do admit to treating him with this unknown drug," I said.

"Dr. Brady, this drug may be unknown to you and your colleague Dr. Reed, but it's not unknown to us here at Blue Lake. This is an often-utilized drug, a combination of an antidepressant, a mood stabilizer, and an antipsychotic. It's a form of lithium that's been altered chemically to reduce the side effects. It has been effective in a limited number of patients."

"You have your own laboratory on-site for creating medications?"

"Yes. The entire basement is a laboratory."

"And you're able to create drugs, get FDA approval, and manufacture them as well?"

"Oh, heavens no. We develop a drug, then we go through the lengthy approval process for experimentation in the form of a drug study. If the drug is eventually approved by the FDA, we'll have partners in the manufacturing sector that we turn over that process to. We merely develop the drug. Another company handles the busy work of production and distribution."

"That's more or less how you handle prescription refills, turn it over to the local docs, correct?"

He paused. "Yes, to some degree. Understand please, that we are in the business of trying to heal patients, and part of that process is to develop new medications for their illnesses. We would have no time for our real mission if we spent all our time manufacturing drugs and writing prescriptions. We have several components to our process, and over time that has worked well for us."

"Is that it for Hubert Brown, Dr. Watson?"

"Essentially. He was discharged after three months, on Equiliminbital only, and according to my records, was not readmitted."

"That would coincide with what his former wife told me. What about the others, if you please?"

He looked through the next file. "Delores White was admitted here twelve years ago in a manic phase of bipolar disorder. She had similar treatment to Mr. Brown. Sedation, ECT, followed by psychotherapy and medication adjustments. She eventually responded well to Equiliminbital and was discharged with a thirty-day supply. She was not readmitted.

"Next, Noni Berry, eighteen years old, who arrived here five years ago at the age of thirteen with a severe case of bipolar disorder. She was in a severe manic state, on multiple medications, and hypertensive with a cardiac arrythmia. She had a seizure upon admission, due to her high blood pressure. She underwent ECT as well and went through extensive medication adjustment. The records indicate she was eventually discharged on Equiliminbital along with five other medications necessary to control her bipolar disorder.

"Last, Freddie Simons. He was admitted here three years ago with a similar condition to Ms. Berry. He required ECT, extensive psychotherapy, and multiple medication changes. He was discharged on a total of four medications, including Equiliminbital."

"It sounds to me, Dr. Watson, that younger patients have a more severe form of the disorder and require more extensive medications than older folks," I said.

"That's true to a degree. What is interesting is that age seems to mitigate the symptoms. Older patients seem to get by on less medication, but we don't have a handle yet on why that happens. We are actively researching that phenomenon, however."

The room was eerily silent for a moment or two. "This is the first contact you've had with anyone involved with the murder of these four patients?" I asked.

"Yes, sir, that's correct," responded administrator McIntyre.

"Would either of you have any idea whatsoever why four former patients, all on the same drug, would have been murdered?"

McIntyre and Watson looked at each other, and McIntyre answered. "None whatsoever. My first response without further information would be that the killings were completely random. Dr. Brady, and Dr. Reed, are you aware of the extent of the use of psychiatric medications?"

Jerry and I shook our heads.

"We estimate that one-sixth of the population of the United States takes some form of psychiatric medication. That's close to 55 million people taking anything from seizure medication to sleeping pills to psychotropic medication, not including medications for the cessation of smoking, and drugs to reduce the symptoms of alcoholism. That's upward of 65 million folks on some sort of medication to mitigate a mental health problem. Looking at the numbers, statistical analysis would reveal that the murders in question are more likely random than having any other cause."

"I just find that hard to believe," I said. "Four people, different ages and from different walks of life, have two things in common. One, a hospitalization at Blue Lake, and two, they were taking the same medication for bipolar disorder."

"I would add two other items, Dr. Brady. They were all murdered with a similar weapon, a hatchet-like object, and they were murdered in the rear of a convenience store. I'm curious how law enforcement would think differently about these four cases if the victims had NOT been hospitalized at Blue Lake and were NOT on psychotropic medication. I think without a doubt that the perpetrator would be labeled a serial killer, and the investigation would take an entirely different track."

"That may be true, Dr. McIntyre, but the fact remains that all four had been treated here and shared a common treatment medication for their disorder. Can either of you tell me if Equiliminbital was a medication developed here at Blue Lake?"

McIntyre and Watson glanced at each other, then Watson answered.

"Yes, it was. It was originally used in an experimental drug program. It was not approved by the FDA for quite some time. Then it was approved, then it was taken off the market. Then it was placed back on the market for limited use with certain diagnostic criteria. We then sold the patent and the manufacturing and distribution rights to a pharmaceutical company for more money than we could imagine, which has helped fund the expansion of our building and the day-to-day operations of this facility."

"And this is your current procedure for the development of new medications?"

"Yes, although we have better attorneys and smarter representatives than we used to. We get an up-front fee for the sale of a new treatment medication after FDA approval, plus a percentage of product sold until the medication reaches the generic phase. Then we're out of the loop on that medication."

"Again, gentlemen, neither of you would have any idea why these four patients of yours would have been targeted and slain?"

Both men shook their heads, and slowly pushed back their chairs and stood.

"It's heartbreaking to hear of these four deaths. We have a vested interest in our patients, to see that they recover from their illnesses and return to being productive members of society. It's especially tragic to hear of the lives of young people being snuffed out long before their time. Neither Dr. Watson nor I have any clue as to why these four people were targeted. Our best guess is they represent random acts of violence upon unsuspecting victims that happened to be former patients of Blue Lake, perpetrated by someone who needs to be in this facility in the worst way."

"Thank you, gentlemen, for your time and for sharing your thoughts. Before we go, I have an acquaintance who has been admitted to your facility, named Bob Jackson. He would be in the drug and alcohol section. I wonder if I might see him before we leave."

Dr. McIntyre left the room and spoke to an assistant at a desk outside the conference room. Dr. Watson stepped over to the coffee pot and poured himself a cup. Shortly, Dr. McIntyre returned. "Dr. Brady, I apologize but he is not available for visitors currently. He was recently admitted, and the staff is worried about delirium tremens setting in, which can be deadly, and as a result he is in the middle of a full-court-press treatment regimen."

"I see. I'm familiar with the problems associated with DTs. I appreciate whatever you can do for him."

Jerry and I shook hands with our hosts and took the elevator down to the lobby.

Once in the car, I asked Jerry what he thought.

"Those two would be great at liar's poker."

"You mean you think they know more than they let on?"

"They both were lying through their pearly whites, in my opinion. One thing on your agenda should be to find out who the prescribers were on all those medication bottles. McIntyre and Watson told us they have physician partners in the local communities that refill prescriptions for Blue Lake patients. Did the same doctor fill those prescriptions, or were multiple doctors involved, would be my first question. Also, I don't understand what Watson said about lithium. I'm familiar with that drug, as it's commonly used for patients with bipolar disorder. He said it had been chemically altered to reduce the side effects when they created Equiliminbital. Also, he implied it took a long time for the drug to get approved by the FDA, then he said it was taken off the market, then reinstated. I think somewhere in all that flowery language lies the answer."

"The answer to what, Jerry?"

"I don't know the question yet, Brady. I must work on the question before I can develop an answer."

"Jerry, I feel I could have been more useful playing golf today than making the trip to Blue Lake. I don't think we discovered any great cover-up by the docs there. McIntyre may be right. The four murders could be random. I had no idea so many people were on psych meds. Did you?"

"Yes, because hardly an autopsy any of us perform at HCMC goes by without seeing the medication sheet from the deceased, and almost everyone is, or has been, on some type of drug, as he said. It's astounding how much medication we Americans take. But I don't believe the murders were random. I think we're missing something, but I don't know what it is yet."

# CHAPTER 17

# PARTY

I dropped Jerry off at HCMC. It was too late to try and join my Friday golf group. While I had nibbled on a pastry and had eaten one finger sandwich, my stomach was growling. I didn't particularly want to go up to my office, as a trip there would probably just produce more work. Better to let Belinda and Maya call me for problems. Mary Louise would still be in Austin, involving herself in one of her charity projects. I was therefore left to my own devices, with hunger pangs increasing by the minute. I had an epiphany and decided that there would be no better way to stimulate my brain into discovering the mystery of the murders than to have Mexican food.

I backtracked from HCMC into Cottonwood Shores and went to Julie's Cocina. I ordered a Dos Equis beer, brewed in Mexico, and a combination plate of a ground beef taco, a ground beef enchilada, and a ground beef tostada. I expected the meal to shorten my life by a few minutes, but at the time it was worth it. I sat outside under an umbrella, away from the madding crowd, and pondered the murder cases over my beer while I waited for food.

I had not talked to Bart Smalls, the boyfriend of Noni Berry. Neither had I spoken to Shannon Wright, the on-and-off girlfriend of Freddie Simons. Perhaps those two could possibly shed some light as to why their paramours had been murdered, although I had no idea what it would be. I also needed to research the prescribing doctors who had partnered, so to speak, with Blue Lake and were writing refills for the four patients who were now dead. Noni had six prescriptions, Freddie had four, and Hubert and Delores each had one. And another issue I had not researched was the occupation of Noni Berry's father. Had Fred Simons not told me that her father was a doctor? Was that even important? Could he have been a prescriber for Blue Lake patients? And what about Equiliminbital? Dr. Watson told us it was a chemically altered form of lithium. How had it been altered? And what were the side effects that the chemists had to try and alter before the second FDA approval?

Thankfully, my food arrived before my mind exploded with unanswered questions. I ordered a second beer, since the first one was history, and dug into some of the best Tex-Mex food around. I had ordered a side of queso, and I carefully spread the thick spicy cheese over all my lunch items and had a feast. By the time I had finished eating and drinking that second beer, all thoughts of investigation were of historical interest only, and I became so somnolent that I almost fell asleep on the drive home.

Tip greeted me with unabashed glee. I took him for a short walk, then collapsed on the bed fully dressed and entered dreamland almost immediately. I awoke to the voice of Mary Louise, who wondered why I was sleeping that time of day with all my clothes on. I had cotton mouth from the beer and Mexican food, so I went into the bathroom, brushed my teeth, gargled, and told her of my day.

She had opened a bottle of Rombauer chardonnay, and I decided that hair of the dog was needed, so I poured myself a glass as well.

"In essence, you don't know any more than you did before you went up there?"

"Correct, except for the concept of local prescribing doctors taking care of Blue Lake patients' refills, and that the clinic is involved in the research and development of psychiatric medications. And that our mystery drug Equiliminbital is essentially just a chemically altered form of lithium, a commonly used drug for bipolar disorder."

"I find that an interesting concept, that they get a drug approved by the FDA then turn it over to another company for mass manufacturing and distribution. They must get a healthy percentage to make it worth their while. There is a lot of money in pharmaceuticals, from what I read."

"I must admit that I don't know much about that side of things. All I hear from my patients is that 'Big Pharma' controls the medication market and how much the prescription drugs cost in the form of insurance deductibles, co-pays, and out-of-pocket expenses."

"On a lighter note, where are you taking me for dinner?"

"Uh, I had not really thought about it. I needed a Julie's fix, so I gorged on Mexican food for lunch."

"I see. Do you think you could muster the energy to take a starving girl to the Yacht Club?"

"For you, my dear, the world is your oyster."

We showered, unfortunately separately. I was convinced Mexican food was an aphrodisiac but was unable to confirm my hypothesis at that time.

It was only a fifteen-minute drive from our home in Granite Falls to the Yacht Club at Horseshoe Bay. The parking lot was full, so I valeted the truck. Upon entry, the greeter told us the dining rooms were packed due to a party we obviously had lost our invitation to, so she sat us in the corner of the bar, which was my favorite seating place anyway. We ordered Tito's dirty vodka martinis and scanned the crowd. I spotted Dr. Buck Owens, my boss in name only, and waved. He returned the wave from across the room, stood, and approached our table.

"How goes it for the Brady family this lovely evening?" he asked.

"Good. You?" I said, watching with amusement as Mary Louise expertly dodged Buck's attempt to taste her luscious red lips, and deflected him artfully to a smooch of her left nostril. She was so good at that maneuver.

"I see you missed the party invitation as well?" Buck said, recovering his pride quickly.

"Yes. What is going on?"

"It's a rehearsal dinner for one of the resort owners' granddaughters. I know the family well enough to speak, but not well enough to get an invitation to a shindig like this. They had a dance floor brought into the ballroom that will hold one hundred and fifty people or so. And do you know who is providing the music? George Strait! Apparently, he's a family friend. I would so love to hear George Strait perform live again. It's been years since I saw him in person. What a great entertainer he is."

"Maybe you can sneak in once everybody is hammered, Buck, and no one will know you're there."

"Fat chance. The security is so tight, you can't enter the ballroom without a key card that was provided in the packet each guest received upon arrival. No, my only hope to hear ol' George is from afar."

"Who is the lucky lady tonight?"

Buck's wife of many years had passed away a while back, and he was in the habit of courting available women about town, young and old.

"My hairdresser. She's a spring chicken, as far as I'm concerned. She's in her forties. By the way, missed you at golf today. Were you working?"

"Not at my job. Maybe I told you, but I'm doing some investigative work into the four recent hatchet murders for Sheriff Joan Wilcox. That led Jerry Reed and me to take a morning drive to a psych facility in Austin called Blue Lake and meet with the hospital administrator and a psychiatrist."

"I wonder if Bill Watson is still there?" Buck asked.

"If that person is Dr. William Watson, chief of psychiatry, then yes. That's who we met with. How do you know him?"

"Brady, I know just about everybody that needs to be known. He and I were classmates in medical school. He was a genius, maybe still is. He had undergraduate degrees in chemistry and pharmacology, then went to med school and became a shrink. I think he was always more interested in the chemical side of psychiatry than the psychotherapy side of things. As I understand, he developed some treatment medications and made a bundle on patent sales. I haven't seen him in years."

"I would say you're correct, Buck. Jerry and I met with him and Seth McIntyre, the administrator. They attributed these four murders to simply random killings and told us that over 50 million Americans are taking some form of psychotropic drug. Even though all four victims had been treated at their institution and were on medications prescribed by their doctors, both physicians felt that the murders were most likely random."

"H-m-m-m. Did you ever consider they might know more than you and Reed, an orthopedic surgeon and a pathologist? That they might be right? I mean, Watson was valedictorian of our med school class, and he's been in the psych business for close to forty years. He probably knows what he's talking about. Listen, I need to get back to my date. Mary Louise, always a pleasure," he said, and walked away.

Our food came, a medium-rare filet for Mary Louise, a shrimp salad for me. We each had a glass of Newton unfiltered chardonnay with our meal, then strolled toward the ballroom. The doors were open, and patrons from the dining areas were streaming in to take their seats. Three large, beefy security men closed the doors once the attendees had checked in, and we were left standing outside like two kids who had missed the bus to school. But then George and his Ace in the Hole Band cranked up the tune "Amarillo by Morning," and we slow-danced outside the ballroom doors like we were part of the crowd. We then two-stepped to "All My Exes Live in Texas," and again slow-danced to "You're Something Special to Me."

Mary Louise danced by herself all the way to the valet. We boarded our chariot and headed home, she still moving to the remembrance of the hit sounds from George Strait and his band. Once we arrived, she began disrobing in stages, strewing clothing from the garage entry door all the way to her bathroom. I picked up behind her, walked Tip, then went into my bathroom and cleaned up a little, brushed my teeth, and gargled. I walked into the bedroom, noted Tip in his bed in the corner, and Mary Louise completely nude lying on the bed on top of the covers.

"I know you think that Mexican food is an aphrodisiac, Jim Bob. Show me what you got, big boy," she said.

And I certainly did.

# CHAPTER 18

# SHANNON AND J. J.

I could not wait to get to the golf course Saturday. I had missed both days the prior weekend doing interviews with family members of the deceased, and the Friday game because of my trip to Blue Lake, which may or may not have been productive. My swing was a little rusty due to what amounted to a two-week layoff, but I could read the putts and was able to contribute to the team score, so my group won a few bucks. We had played the Summit Ridge, a Nicklaus signature design course, and while we were sitting outside having a post-competition beverage, Buck Owens pulled me aside.

"I got a call from my old friend Bill Watson this morning. Seems you might have ruffled some feathers during your visit to Blue Lake."

"I told you about the trip last night at the Yacht Club."

"I know, but I had had a few cocktails, so I didn't pay close attention. He implied that you were accusatory, implying that somehow Blue Lake and its doctors were responsible for the murders of four of its patients."

"That is absolutely not true. Jerry Reed was with me the entire time. We asked questions about the patients, and about medications, and about refilling prescriptions. We were very polite and had no intention of ruffling any feathers, as you called it. On the other hand, perhaps we touched on a nerve, and they have some vague culpability but were reluctant to share what that might be. There could be liability involved on behalf of the victims' families if it were proven that Blue Lake somehow contributed to the deaths of their loved ones. But I didn't bring anything like that up with the two doctors."

"Well, Bill was a little defensive, talked about Blue Lake's success in treating the mentally ill, and how much they have done for the community, and the medications they've developed, and on and on. Although Bill is an old friend of mine, and prominent in the world of psychiatry, I felt he was overstating his position. I tend to agree with you, although I hate to admit that. You've become involved in some messes in the past that ultimately involved me, and I can't say I've enjoyed the notoriety."

"I appreciate your support. I'm going to touch base with Sheriff Wilcox and Susan Beeson, apprise them of my findings, and see if they want me to continue or turn it over to the authorities and the real investigators. I can't prove it, but I have a feeling in my gut that this will not turn out well, and I want to be detached from it when the proverbial shit hits the fan."

"Smart man. Let me know what the powers that be say."

"Will do."

I called Joan Wilcox from the car after Saturday golf and told her of our trip to Blue Lake and described the skimpy findings Jerry and I managed to come up with.

"So, no smoking gun?" she asked.

"Not that we could see, but both Jerry and I think that the two doctors we spoke to were keeping some information to themselves. I cannot prove that, but I have a feeling that there is something lurking beneath the surface. What do you want me to do at this point?"

"What do you feel comfortable doing?"

"For the purpose of completion, I would like to speak to Shannon Wright, the on-again off-again girlfriend of Freddie Simons. I seem to recall Freddie's dad told me Shannon's father was a doctor. I'm not sure if that has anything to do with the murders, however. Also, I'd like to talk to Bart Smalls, former boyfriend of Noni Berry. Last, I'd like to check out the prescription-writers for refills on the four deceased victims. That may or may not lead to anything. Other than those issues, I don't know what else I can do to help you. Susan Beeson might be a good addition to your investigation team, especially if there's another murder."

"Oh, God, I hope not. That's all I need right now."

I pulled onto the frontage road of Highway 71, looked through my paperwork, and found a cell phone number for Shannon Wright. I called, got a recorded message, and left her my number and asked her to please return my call. I found a number for the household, called that number, and a woman answered.

"This is Dr. Jim Brady. With whom am I speaking please?"

"Shannon Wright."

"Perfect. I just left you a message to call me. I'm assisting the authorities in the investigation of Freddie Simons's murder, and I have a few questions to ask you. Would you be available? I'm returning home from golf in Horseshoe Bay, so you're not far away."

She hesitated for a moment, then said, "I guess it's okay."

"Good. See you in ten minutes or so."

I made a U-turn, took a shortcut on Summit Ridge Parkway to FM 2147, then drove up the hill and entered the gated enclave of Applehead Island. The security guard took down my license plate number as well as my name and address. Fortunately, Shannon had called ahead to grant my permission to enter. I wandered through a myriad of houses perched on the water with boat docks housing a minimum of two boats. I found the address, exited the truck, and knocked on the door.

Shannon Wright wore white shorts and a blue tank top, and she was barefoot. Her blond hair was long, and she had gathered it into a ponytail that almost reached her waist. She invited me in and led me to a great room with a wall of windows overlooking Lake LBJ, and we sat in chintz chairs opposite a glass coffee table.

"So how did you know Freddie?" she asked.

"I didn't know him. I spoke to his father as part of the investigation into Freddie's death, and he gave me your name. Mr. Simons suggested you and his son had an intermittent relationship over quite a long period of time, and that you also had been a patient at Blue Lake."

She sighed deeply. "Freddie was the love of my young life, but I just didn't realize it until it was too late. We were high school friends, then intermittent lovers. My parents encouraged me to break it off with Freddie, citing that his dad worked for the post office and Freddie was a trainee for the HEB chain's management program, and that his family just was not good enough for the Wright family. It just about killed Freddie when he failed the physical to get into the army. He went into full manic mode when that happened, which is how he ended up in Blue Lake.

"My parents finally left me alone when it came to Freddie, their logic being that I was going to UT and would quickly outgrow Freddie Simons. Well, let me tell you this. After two years in Austin, Freddie had never looked better. It seemed that every boy I dated tried to fight me for the bathroom mirror. So, we struck up our relationship again when I came home for breaks. I think my parents were deathly afraid that I would get pregnant, and they would be left with a grandchild with two crazy-people genes."

"Would you have any idea whatsoever why someone would want to kill Freddie?"

She shook her head. "No. Freddie was a kind man to everyone, not just to a supervisor or someone who might do him some good career-wise. He was a gentle soul. He was afflicted with this terrible disorder, as am I, but the meds he was on kept him very level from an emotional standpoint. He was able to function normally, even did well in HEB's management trainee program. Most of us with bipolar disorder have ups and downs to the extent we cannot function in normal society. But Freddie was doing well. And then . . ."

"I don't know if you've heard about the three other murders, but Freddie was the fourth in a series of folks with bipolar disorder who had been hospitalized at Blue Lake who were murdered."

"Yes, I heard about the others, but I can't imagine why. Unless . . ."

"Unless what, Shannon?"

"Well, when you're in lockdown with a bunch of other people with mental disorders just like yourself, there is serious talk about everything . . . suicide, medications, the future of your life. We feel more comfortable opening our souls to someone facing the same everyday problems, more so than to the so-called normal people who are there to treat us. What I'm saying is, those affected talk to each other."

"Was there some sort of conversation while you were an inpatient about anything irregular at Blue Lake?"

"Just rumors."

"About what?"

"About someone who had escaped."

"From Blue Lake?"

"Yes. I was there over a year ago. That's when I heard about it from a fellow inpatient."

"What was the significance of a patient escaping? Were they not caught?"

"I don't know about his capture or not, but the rumor was that the guy was older than the crowd I hung out with there. That he had an unusual shape to his body and his face, and the talk was that he had killed an attendant in the process of escaping."

Shannon didn't have much else to reveal. I thanked her for her time and left.

I called the number for Bart Smalls that was in the paperwork Joan Wilcox had given me. When he answered I could barely hear him, due to almost deafening rock music of some sort in the background.

"Bart, this is Dr. Brady. I'd like to talk to you about Noni. Please turn the music down."

"Who is this?" he said slurring his words after the noise subsided.

"Dr. Jim Brady. I'm helping the authorities investigate the deaths of the four Blue Lake patients of which Noni your girlfriend was one."

"Yeah, man, what a drag that was, finding her in the trunk of the car. Dude, she had been hit hard in the head, blood everywhere. I still cannot believe it. Why her? She was a cool chick, never did nobody wrong."

I would have preferred to interview him in person, but with his family history, I thought it best to stay away from the Smallses' home. "Did she ever express worries of any kind, that her life might be in danger, anything like that?"

"No, man, nothing like that. I had been around her a time or two when she went a little nuts on me, and other times when she was so depressed that she talked about offing herself, but then she would take her pills and level out. She was a cool chick. I miss her, man."

The music, if you want to call it that, ratcheted back up, and then the line went dead. So much for Bart Smalls. He would be unreliable for gathering most any kind of information, and I thought I could cross him off my list of people who could contribute to solving these murder cases.

I called Mary Louise and told her I was on my way home. She said we would have guests for dinner. When I asked who, she said it was a surprise.

Tip did not greet me when I arrived home, which was unusual. And then I heard child sounds in the background and realized my first and only grandchild, J. J. Jr., was in the house. He was a little over two years old, with hair so blond it was almost white. He was sitting in Mary Louise's lap while she read him a story. J. J., our only son, was standing at the bar, pouring himself a beer and watching the proceedings between his mother and his son.

"Hey, Pop," he said, hugging me. Either he had become taller, or I was shrinking. He was lean as always, with a muscular upper body.

"This is a nice surprise. What are you doing in our neck of the woods?"

"I had to make a trip to Austin for meetings, so I thought we'd detour here for a night or two."

J. J. and his college roommate Brad Broussard had started a detective agency of sorts while in school, which had blossomed into an internationally known company known as B&B Investigations. The company did investigation work for private companies, but also did work for governmental agencies and law enforcement agencies in the field of cybercrime. J. J. ran the firm's branch in Dallas, while Brad handled the Houston office.

"It's great to see you, son. I wonder if I could pry my grandson out of your mother's lap for a hug?"

He stared at me for a moment, then said, "No way."

Mary Louise was having a love affair with our grandson. She had even suggested having a second home in Dallas so we could be with him more often. I had not acted on that for many reasons, but mainly because of the looks we had gotten from J. J. and his wife Kathryn when she mentioned that idea aloud. We loved our daughter-in-law a great deal, as she did us, but our relationship was best enjoyed from a distance.

"Did Kathryn come as well?"

"No, she has bank meetings on Monday morning, and she cannot miss those. My meeting is Monday morning, so I thought I'd leave Junior here with Mom and pick him up after the meeting and drive back to Dallas in the afternoon."

"I think your mother would be happy to take him for a week, maybe a month."

My grandson finally realized I was home and ran over to greet me with a hug to my knees, then ran back to Nana's lap. J. J. and I had a nice visit. Mary Louise had prepared J. J.'s favorite, blackened salmon, with new potatoes, green beans, cauliflower, and rice pudding for dessert. The boys cleaned up the dishes while Nana bestowed much-needed attention on Junior. As she read a multitude of stories to him, J. J. and I retreated to the terrace for an after-dinner libation. He had brought along a new after-dinner drink for us to try.

"Pop, are you spending your time working at your real job of surgeon, or have you involved yourself in some sort of investigative activity?"

"I still have a busy practice with surgery Monday and Wednesday, and clinic patients Tuesday and Thursday. I try to reserve Friday and Saturday for golf, unless an emergency comes in, and Sundays for whatever your mother wants to do. She's taken up golf, and mostly we'll go out and play nine holes Sunday, and depending on our tee time, have lunch or dinner at the club. As you know, I keep my finger in the detective-work pie when possible. In fact, I was asked by Sheriff Joan Wilcox to work on solving a series of murders. It seems there's a miscreant out there who's attacked and killed four local citizens using a hatchet. All four were killed in the rear refuse area of convenience stores. During the process of interviewing family members of each victim, I discovered that each carried a diagnosis of bipolar disorder, had been hospitalized at Blue Lake Psychiatric Hospital in Austin, and had been prescribed the same medication for their disorder.

"I went up there yesterday with Dr. Jerry Reed, chief pathologist at HCMC, and interviewed the hospital administrator and the chief of psychiatry. We didn't learn much, other than to confirm that each victim had been a patient there at one time or another."

"What did those guys have to say about the murders?"

"They suggested the murders were completely random, citing that 55 million Americans are on some sort of psychiatric drug, and that the hospital could not be responsible for the deaths of four former patients."

"Interesting. I think they're hiding something."

"That's exactly what Jerry said."

"Mind if I look into it?"

"What? Blue Lake?"

"Yes. I might pull the files, check out the murder locations, look at Blue Lake's history. I have access to a lot of data, you know."

"I do. Your access is not always legal, though, is it?"

"Pop, B&B Investigations is a highly respected company specializing in obtaining information about people and businesses that said people and businesses want to stay hidden but which my clients do not. We provide a valuable service to private individuals, corporations, and governmental and law enforcement entities."

"You did not answer my question."

"No, sir, I did not."

"Well, let me say that one of the people I interviewed was the girlfriend of one of the victims, and while she had been at Blue Lake, there was a rumor going round that a patient had escaped and had killed an attendant during the process. While you're looking into these aspects of the case, you might keep that in mind. And remember that you volunteered to investigate these murders which, I assume, includes looking into the Blue Lake facility. I didn't ask, nor did I hire you to involve yourself in this murky business."

"This one's on me, Pop."

"I'm curious as to what about these cases interests you so."

"I hate to see a wrong not righted, and I hate to see young life snuffed out by a violent act accompanied by an unsolved mystery. I just have a gut feeling that the hospital knows more than they divulged to you and is hiding something. I inherited my suspicious nature from you, Pop."

"Any assistance you can provide, son, will be most welcome. Now about this brandy . . ."

# CHAPTER 19

# PRESCRIPTIONS AND A VISITOR

I tossed and turned that night and could not get to sleep. I finally got out of bed, poured myself a stiff single-malt scotch, and went into my office. I pulled out all the pill bottles that I had accumulated. There was only the spelled version of Delores White's prescription, as her aunt was unable to find the actual medication. I had Hubert Brown's single bottle, six bottles from Noni Berry, and Freddie Simons's four bottles.

I first looked at the locations of where the prescriptions were filled. Hubert had filled his Equiliminbital at Walmart on the northern end of Marble Falls on Highway 281.

Freddie had filled his four prescriptions at HEB, logical because he worked at the store, and it was the most convenient location for him, most likely.

I had no location for Delores's prescription.

Noni had filled her six medications at Bayside Pharmacy, located in Horseshoe Bay and closest to her home.

I then looked at the prescribing doctors for each prescription. Dr. Theo Strong had prescribed Hubert's only medication, Equiliminbital. I had no idea about Delores's prescribing doctor. Three of Freddie's prescriptions were filled by Dr. Millicent

Hastings, but his Equiliminbital had been prescribed by . . . Dr. Theo Strong. A coincidence? I looked through Noni's pill bottles and discovered that five of the six medications were prescribed by Dr. Stanley Howser, but the Equiliminbital had been prescribed by, once again, Dr. Theo Strong. I wondered what in the world that was about.

It was 3 a.m. and too early to call, but I had to find out from the parents of Noni Berry and the father of Freddie Simons about the prescription issue. Why was one specific doctor prescribing their Equiliminbital, and another prescribing the other medications?

Suspicious thoughts ran through my head, and I realized that my review of the medications was not a sleep inducer. I poured another scotch and pondered. I must have drifted off to sleep, because I woke up to daylight, a stiff neck, and sounds and smells coming from the kitchen.

Junior was in his highchair and had scattered more food onto the floor than into his mouth. He was giggling and banging his spoon onto the plastic tray as he watched Tip scarf up his leftovers.

"Couldn't sleep?" Mary Louise asked.

"No, and I didn't want to wake you, so I had a couple of scotches and reviewed some paperwork I had. That didn't help."

"Sorry. Listen, I know this is Sunday, but I want to spend the day with Junior. Is that okay?"

"Of course. You get to see me all the time, him not so often. What are you going to do?"

"After I get him fed, and then the rest of us fed, I thought I'd take him over to the pool at the club. It's heated and has a very shallow section, so it would be safe for him. You're welcome to go with us."

"I might. I have a few phone calls to make. Is J. J. up?"

"Yes, he came in and got his coffee, saw that Junior was well taken care of, and returned to his quarters."

Tip was annoyed that Junior was the center of attention, so he kept nudging me. I fed him his breakfast and wandered out back with him. The water was clear blue, with a few fishermen out casting their lines in hopes of a bite. Tip's ears perked up and he barked once, a sign of trouble. I wandered over to where he was, and he was intently staring into the far corner of the backyard. There was something there, huddled between the conjunction of the two three-foot walls. I thought it was an animal of some sort, then the creature unfurled itself and stood. It looked like a boy or a small man with strawberry blond hair. He was filthy and smelled, even from that distance. He appeared to have a spinal curvature, like severe scoliosis combined with a severe kyphosis. He limped as he walked toward me. As he neared me, I caught the glint of an object in his right hand, and it appeared to be a hatchet.

Tip whined, turned, and ran toward the house, leaving me to die at the hands of . . . whoever this was.

I didn't know what to do, so I simply said, "Hello."

By then he was about ten feet away, and I could see his facial and orbital bones were uneven and pronounced.

"Hungry," he said.

"I can get you some food. Wait here."

I walked backward into the kitchen, grabbed some toast and a few slices of bacon, and started my return to the backyard. Mary Louise had been watching through the window.

"Want me to call somebody?" she asked.

"Yes. Sheriff Joan, STAT. I may have her killer here."

I walked back into the yard to within a few feet of my visitor and handed him the breakfast items. He grabbed them with his left hand, taking care to keep his weapon ready in his right hand.

He gobbled the food down ravenously, dropped some, then picked it up off the ground, sat down, and hungrily ate it.

"More," he said.

I returned to the kitchen, Mary Louise handed me more breakfast treats, and I went back out and handed our guest the food and sat down on the ground as well. I watched him eat hungrily, then we sat in silence for a while.

"What is your name?" I asked.

"Philip," he said.

"Do you have a last name?"

"Don't remember."

"Where do you live?"

"Nowhere. Everywhere."

"Do you have any family, a mother or father?"

"Not anymore. Dead. But I 'scaped."

"You escaped? From where?"

"That place. I was locked up there. Mama died there."

"Do you remember the name of the place?"

"No."

He got up, turned away, and walked toward the fence.

"Why are you here? Did you come to see me?"

"Yes. Shannon told me."

"Shannon Wright? How do you know her?"

"From the place. She said you could help me."

I felt movement behind me and saw Sheriff Joan and a deputy walk into the backyard.

Philip kept walking toward the fence, then started to run. Both Joan and her deputy ran after him, but he was lightning quick, jumping over the fence at warp speed. The two jumped over the fence after him and scoured the raw landscape that led down the hill to Lake LBJ, but they were unable to find my visitor.

Joan returned, out of breath. "Was that my killer?"

"Well, he had a hatchet. He seemed to have a cognitive deficit of some sort, and a severe spinal and facial distortion, probably from birth. But he came looking for me, he said."

"Why you, and how in the world did he find you?"

"He said Shannon told him. The only Shannon I know is Shannon Wright, Freddie Simons's former girlfriend, with whom I spoke only yesterday. She told me there were rumors when she was an inpatient at Blue Lake of an escapee who had killed someone during his exit. Sounds like she knows more than she let on."

"Do you think she's helping this guy or what?"

"I don't know, but I think we should pay her another visit."

Sheriff Joan Wilcox made the call to the Wright house and told the mother that we would be dropping by shortly, and in case Shannon had any plans, to cancel them.

Joan offered me a ride in her squad car to save the planet a few gallons of gasoline emissions, but I declined. My plan was to join Mary Louise at the pool after the interviews ended.

We arrived at the Wright house, knocked, and were admitted by Shannon's mother, name of Beverly. She appeared to be in her mid-forties, attractive, tall, and thin, with her hair in a scarf. She introduced us to Shannon's father, Dr. Charles Wright, an internal medicine specialist who worked out of the Hill Country Medical Center. He and I didn't know each other, regardless of the fact we worked in the same facility. He was several inches taller than me, with a shaved head, and he wore glasses.

"What is this about?" asked Dr. Wright.

"Dr. Brady was here yesterday and interviewed your daughter. And before either of you ask why he, an orthopedic surgeon, is involved in the investigation of the recent four murders, he's been acting under the auspices of the sheriff's department of Burnet County and with the approval of the FBI out of Austin. We are here to speak to your daughter Shannon, who apparently has a relationship with an escaped inpatient of Blue Lake who may be the killer of four people who also were patients at Blue Lake at one time," Sheriff Joan orated.

"I think she's still sleeping," said Beverly.

"Wake her up, Mrs. Wright. This is important. You don't want to hinder this investigation, do you?"

"Of course not," she said, and left the room.

"Have a seat," said Dr. Wright. "I've worked at HCMC for quite some time, and I don't think we've ever met, Dr. Brady."

"My tenure there is probably much shorter than yours, only a few years now. I practiced in Houston at the University Medical Center for most of my career."

"I see. Most of my practice is in the office these days. What with hospitalists taking over the care of patients that get admitted, there's no longer room for the family doctor/internist in the hospital setting. There are good and bad aspects to that form of treatment, but it's the wave of the future. In the old days, if I had a sick patient, I would admit them, care for them, make rounds on them daily, and sometimes twice daily. I was able to keep current with all the new docs coming in to HCMC, keep my finger in the hospital pie, so to speak. Now it's like I'm a stranger over there."

Before I could comment, a sleepy Shannon Wright arrived. She curled up on the couch next to her dad and looked at Joan and I sullenly.

"Shannon, I am Sheriff Joan Wilcox. Dr. Brady here paid you a visit yesterday because of your relationship with Freddie Simons. You mentioned a rumor that was going around when you were an inpatient at Blue Lake about an escaped inpatient with, I believe you called it a differently shaped body, who might have killed an attendant during the process of the escape. This morning, a man fitting that description showed up in Dr. Brady's backyard, wielding a hatchet, asking for food, and told Dr. Brady that you had sent him there for help. I'd like to hear more about that. This man could well be the murderer we're looking for and may well have killed your boyfriend as well as three other people. Why you would be protecting him, I'd very much like to know."

Shannon leaned into her dad and sobbed.

"I met Philip when I was at Blue Lake a couple of years ago. People didn't react well to him because of his appearance. He took a liking to me, for whatever reason, but he went around acting like he was going to kill his fellow inmates with a pretend hammer or something in his right hand. We had a couple of group sessions together, then later during my stay there something bad happened and he was put in lockdown. I didn't see him for a month or so, then the next time I did he was so drugged up that he could barely speak. We talked briefly, and he kept insisting he had to get out of there. That the doctors had killed his mother, and that they were going to kill him as well.

"Before I was discharged, I wrote down my cell phone number and my address and told him that if he got out and needed help, he could call me."

"Shannon! What were you thinking?" her mother shouted. "Bringing a murderer into our home? Have you lost your . . . ?"

"Mind, mother. And yes, I lost my mind a long time ago."

"Shannon," said Joan, redirecting the conversation, "you're the only person we have knowledge of who was a patient at Blue Lake, taking bipolar medication, who has not been attacked or murdered. Do you know of any other former patients in the area we could talk to? Or why Philip would be targeting former patients in the first place? Seems to me his problem is with the institution, not the patients."

"I can't answer that. His mind is not wired like normal. And I don't know anyone else from around here that has been hospitalized at Blue Lake. My parents were gone yesterday, so Philip came over. I let him take a shower, gave him some food, and told him to turn himself in to the authorities. He was carrying that stupid hatchet around, and where he got that I have no idea. He probably stole it from a hardware store, or from someone's garage."

"How about information as to how he might have obtained identities of the victims and discovered their locations around various convenience stores?"

"Not a clue, Sheriff. Sorry. You're acting like he's for sure the killer."

"He may be a friend of yours, but if you had seen his victims' head wounds, you wouldn't be so cavalier about the matter. Did he ever mention to you if he got out of Blue Lake that he would find his former fellow patients and do them bodily harm? And for what reason?"

"No, he never said anything of that nature to me."

"I have a question for any of you regarding the filling of your medication," I said. "Noni Berry had six prescriptions. Five were refilled by a local doctor by the name of Dr. Stanley Howser, and one, the Equiliminbital, was refilled by Dr. Theo Strong. Your friend Freddie had four prescriptions, three refilled by Dr. Millicent Hastings, and again, his Equiliminbital filled by Dr. Theo Strong. How many medications are you on, Shannon, and who fills your medication?"

"I take three different meds, and my dad refills them for me. He is a doctor, you know."

"I understand. Do you take Equiliminbital?"

"I take Risperdal, Depakote, and Symbyax. I don't take that other drug you mentioned."

"Dr. Wright, do you have any idea why a different doctor would be refilling the deceased patients' Equiliminbital?"

"Not really, Dr. Brady. Some medications have a different classification from others, especially when it comes to narcotics. The DEA has established the Controlled Substances Schedule I through Schedule V, with Schedules II through V containing the commonly authorized medications that a practitioner can prescribe. Schedule I drugs would be those that traditionally are associated with a high-percentage chance of addiction, and to be of questionable medical value, such as heroin, LSD, and marijuana. I don't understand why this Equiliminbital would be in a Schedule I class, but I guess it's possible. Maybe this Dr. Strong has a Schedule I permit, and he's the only one in the area authorized to prescribe it. But again, I'm not familiar with that medication."

"Well, all four of the victims were taking Equiliminbital, and three of the four had been prescribed that medication by Dr. Theo Strong. I was at Blue Lake yesterday and spoke to the chief of psychiatry and the hospital administrator. They both implied that Equiliminbital was at one time an experimental drug, and was approved, then disapproved, then re-approved by the FDA. The two doctors I spoke to also told me that Equiliminbital was a product of chemically modified lithium, designed to control symptoms of bipolar disorder. Why would Dr. Strong be prescribing a Schedule I narcotic in the form of a chemically modified lithium to control bipolar disorder? Is he a psychiatrist? Was he a treating physician of the victims?"

No one in the room spoke, so I assumed there were no more answers to be had at the Wright residence.

Sheriff Joan stood, thanked the family for their time, and we departed.

# CHAPTER 20

# JUNIOR

I parked in a member-only parking spot near the club entry and wandered along the sidewalks back to the pool area, where I found my bride and my grandson frolicking in the very shallow end of the pool. The area was quiet for a Sunday morning.

"Solve any great mysteries, husband?"

"I seem to be creating more mysteries than solving any. How does Junior like the water?"

"He loves it. Did you bring your suit?"

"No, I forgot. In the turmoil of the morning . . ."

"Too bad. Take your shoes off and sit poolside so Junior will know you're participating in our outing."

I thought of all sorts of retorts to her comment, but I thought better of it and did as I was instructed. Not being much on child psychology, I would not want my grandson's psyche to be ruined by my lack of participation in the swimfest. Besides, the water was nice and warm, and quite pleasant on the senses, and prompted my concerns about murder, medications, and psychiatrists to ebb.

When we returned home, we found a note from J. J. that he had left early for Austin and would return Monday afternoon to pick up Junior and return to Dallas. I could see the sadness in

Mary Louise's eyes, but she said nothing. He included in the note for me to call him that evening if I had a chance. We constructed sandwiches with leftover blackened salmon, bagels, and cream cheese and pretended the lunch was a breakfast with lox. I was not sure what sort of substance Junior was eating, but it had a creamy texture and was easy to toss around once he had loaded it onto a spoon. I made the mistake of accentuating my dodging of Junior's thrown food because he thought that was hilarious and therefore continued to throw bits of slop in my direction. Mary Louise stopped the game once Junior and I—as well as the floor—were covered with debris, and hauled him off for a bath, clean clothes, and a nap.

I sat in my office and stared out at the lake for a bit, then did a computer search for Dr. Theo Strong. According to the Texas State Medical Board, he was a board-certified psychiatrist and had two offices, one in the Bee Cave area of Austin, the other in Marble Falls. He had written many articles on various psychiatric subjects, mostly to do with bipolar disorder. He had trained at the University of Texas Medical Branch in Galveston and had done his residency and fellowship at the Menninger Clinic in Kansas. He had also done post-graduate training at Blue Lake Psychiatric Hospital, so he did have a connection there. As far as I could tell, his credentials were impeccable on paper.

The study of Dr. Theo Strong, combined with the after-effects of lunch, induced sleepiness, so I planted myself in my recliner and was soon asleep. I didn't know how much time had passed, but I awoke to the sounds of a baby in the house, which was screeching, laughing, and crying, interspersed with the yelling of "No!" like only a two-year-old can muster.

I wandered into the great room and saw Junior and Mary Louise huddled together watching a cartoon on television starring a little girl named Dora. I checked the clock and found it was just past 4 p.m., late enough for a beer, but too early for a cocktail . . . although, it was five o'clock somewhere. I opted for a cold beer and sat next to Mary Louise as Junior gyrated to the sounds of music from the show, which I learned was *Dora the Explorer*.

"Would you like an adult beverage?" I asked.

"Yes, but I'd like to be a responsible grandmother, so I must decline. This child is wearing me out. I love him to death, but how in the world did we handle this when J. J. was a baby? I'll have to sleep for days after he leaves."

"Young children are for young parents. We are supposed to keep grandchildren for a day or two, spoil them rotten, then return the little darlings to their parents, completely and totally off their routine. And then laugh about it when the parents complain. It's the way of the world, or so I have read."

"You are so bad. What do you want to do about dinner?"

"I can pick something up if you like. I don't think Junior is restaurant material yet."

"That's the truth. He might like a pizza at home, though."

"Yep. Think of the mess he could make with that!"

We agreed on pizza. I ordered takeout from Restaurant 360, just down the road from us and hard to beat in flavor and portions. I ordered pepperoni and Margherita pizzas and garlic bread sticks, and as usual ordered too much, leaving plenty for a late-night snack.

As expected, Junior made an absolute mess of his pepperoni pizza, with pieces of meat and crust thrown far and wide. He had one heck of an arm for a two-year-old and I briefly dreamed of him as a starting college quarterback or a major league pitcher. Then reality sank in as he lofted a spoonful of partially chewed gruel directly into Nana's hair, which did not sit particularly well with the matron of the house. In a move that would make any running back proud, she hoisted Junior out of his chair, tossed his spoon into the sink, and made for the bathroom. I could hear screeching interspersed with "No's" being yelled, but order was finally restored in the Brady household. The only member of the family that seemed to be happy was Tip, who was busy devouring Junior's leftovers off the floor. Normally I'd have told him to stop, but he was acting like a good vacuum cleaner and was saving me the trouble of cleaning up the mess.

I had made us a couple of Tito's dirty vodka martinis and put them in the freezer during the melee in the bathroom. Once Mary Louise returned to the kitchen, with hair devoid of pizza slop and Junior in his bed, I brought the martinis to the table.

"You're a life saver," she said, as she gulped half of it down in one swallow.

"Remember our discussions about buying a second home in Dallas to be closer to Junior?" she asked.

"Yes, of course. And how that would allow you to see him more often, babysitting him in the evenings and on the weekends while J. J. and Kathryn go have fun."

"Based on today, and what will likely be a repeat tomorrow, I think we are just close enough as it is. Three hours away is about right, I'm now thinking. I raised one child and am too old to raise another."

I didn't say anything, but all I could think about was Garth Brooks and his unanswered prayers.

Mary Louise was exhausted and went to bed before eight o'clock. I called J. J. on his cell phone to see what he had wanted.

"I did some research on Blue Lake today. Interesting institution. They have an enormous endowment, primarily due to the development of various psychiatric medications the firm has invented and patents they have held. It seems they like to develop a new medication, get the patent, get FDA approval for the drug in patients, then sell off the product to a large pharmaceutical company for manufacturing and distribution, while taking an up-front fee and then adding on a surcharge for patient usage. I don't know much about how other firms work, but this seems unique to me. You mentioned you had been to the hospital, I think. Did you see the laboratory?"

"No. All I heard was that it takes up the entire basement of the building, but the principals didn't offer to show the facilities to me."

"I found a few photos online. It's impressive."

"So, what do you think? Nothing that looks like a fly in the ointment?"

"I don't know yet. I need to refine my search. There's not much to find easily. Lots of firewalls and passwords, which is not unusual for a large, successful company. I did find a snippet of information about some trouble they had with a drug for bipolar disorder. Seems it was approved by the FDA, then taken off the market, then put back on the market again."

"Dr. Watson, the chief of psychiatry, mentioned that to me in reference to the drug Equiliminbital. All the victims of the hatchet killer were taking it, which I thought was a big deal but which he said was more likely a coincidence, considering how many people in the country are taking psych meds. I think he said the drug was basically lithium that had been modified chemically and had more effectiveness in controlling the manic side of bipolar disorder but created fewer side effects in accentuating the depression aspect. That's one of the biggest problems with treating bipolar disorder. Drugs that reduce the manic episodes often trigger severe depression. That's why these people often need to take several different medications to control both facets of the disorder. Two of the victims, both of whom were older, were only taking Equiliminbital. The two younger victims were taking multiple medications."

"Pops, I'd imagine that it would be ideal to find one drug only that controlled the disorder. It would be cheaper obviously, and less confusing for the patient, and worth a fortune probably. But there is a reason that hasn't happened."

"That's my advice to you, young man. Follow the money trail. In almost every situation of malfeasance, money holds the key to discovery."

All good things must come to an end, and so it was that the alarm wakened me Monday morning at 5 a.m. with its shrill and obnoxious beeping. The reality of work was about to set in. I arrived at the hospital at 6 a.m. and greeted Belinda at the nurses' station on the orthopedic floor of HCMC.

"Morning, Doc. How was your weekend?"

"We have our almost-two-year-old grandson staying with us."

"Don't say another word. We all know what that's like, don't we?" she said to the nursing staff at the station. There were nods and uh-huhs all around.

"Do we have anyone left on the floor?"

"The five joint replacements and the hip labrum repair from Wednesday all went either home or to rehab. Mr. Ben Harper, with the fractured hip, is still in the hospital but was moved to the medical floor. He had symptoms of coronary occlusion on Thursday night with chest pain and shortness of breath, and he had a couple of stents put in. Also, Matt Solis is still here."

"The kid with the fractured knee? That would be a hospital admission of five nights. The insurance company will never approve that."

"They already did. Turns out he has bipolar disorder and had a full manic attack Friday night. He required sedation and intravenous lithium, and then he crashed emotionally and required antidepressants on Saturday. The shrinks have had a real mess trying to keep him stable."

"Did we know this? That he had bipolar?"

"No. The mother didn't think his psychiatric history was germane to having his knee fixed."

"We could have killed him in the operating room, depending on which drugs the anesthesiologist gave him and their interaction with his bipolar meds."

"Yes, we could have. Beverly, his mother, and I have had several long conversations about that."

"Is she with him?"

"Yes, sir."

We walked down the hallway to the Solis room and found Matt sound asleep and his mother in the same condition in the reclining chair adjacent to the bed. I tapped her on the shoulder. She awoke with a start.

"Oh, Dr. Brady, you scared me. I was dreaming about a Mamas and Papas concert I had attended years ago."

"I'm glad to hear your son is alive, Beverly. Do you realize what a disaster that could have been, the staff not aware of Matt's condition?"

"I do now. I've had several conversations with Belinda about it. I don't know what I was thinking, or was not thinking, for that matter. With all the trouble we've had with Matt and bipolar disorder, I could have precipitated my own son's demise. He's been doing so well lately, since a new medication has been added to his regimen."

"I'm glad for that, at least. In the future, wherever you go for medical care, you absolutely must inform the physicians and nurses about Matt's condition and the medications he's taking."

"I know that now, and I am so sorry," she said, and wept.

"Do you happen to know what medications Matt is currently taking?"

"Yes. I went home Saturday and brought the pill bottles back up. Here they are," she said, reached into her purse and handed me four prescription bottles. Risperdal, Depakote, and Symbyax had been prescribed by his local psychiatrist. The prescribing doctor's name on three bottles was the same, Dr. Millicent Hastings, who happened to be the same prescribing doctor on Freddie Simons's prescriptions. In a small town, I thought that probably it was not unheard of to have two boys around the same age go to the same psychiatrist. The fourth bottle, however, was for Equiliminbital, prescribed by none other than Dr. Theo Strong.

That brought up more questions for me. The victims so far were Hubert Brown, Delores White, Noni Berry, and Freddie Simons. Each were on Equiliminbital. I had learned from Matt Solis's mother that he also was on Equiliminbital. Had he been a target for murder by hatchet? Or was the fact that he was on the drug associated with the victims simply a coincidence? Were there other factors common to the victims that precipitated their demise besides taking the same bipolar medication?

I needed to speak with Dr. Theo Strong, provided he would talk to me. And I wanted to talk to poor Philip again, despite all the things that would be wrong about that.

CHAPTER 21

# PHILIP

I had to put all things bipolar aside and concentrate on my work. We had six cases for Monday, four hip and two knee replacements. All six were virgin cases, no revisions, so the day went smoothly and pleasantly. Belinda and I finished up around 4 p.m., and we dutifully sought out the families and friends of the recently operated on and shared our happiness that the procedures had gone well. We checked on the patients that were in the recovery room, then went upstairs to the orthopedic floor and checked on the patients who had made it to their respective rooms. Those duties took another hour, and we arrived back in my office around 5 p.m. Maya had a few questions to ask me, which I answered easily, then I set about to clean off the paperwork on my desk. As I did, thoughts of mental illness and death by hatchet crept back into my subconscious, and I had to forcefully shove those thoughts out of the way to complete my dictation, sign charts, and return phone calls.

I called it a day at 6 p.m. and decided to get some exercise and walk down the three flights of stairs rather than lazily take the elevator. I had exited the parking garage door and was just about to activate the key fob for my truck when I felt a presence beside me. It was Philip, who again wielded his hatchet, but fortunately didn't seem directed to use it on me.

"Philip," I said. "I'm amazed at your ability to find me, and for that matter, other people you may have come in contact with." I had started to say other people you've murdered, but I didn't want to put myself in jeopardy. So, I said kindly, "How did you locate me?"

"Came last week, so I knew. You shot at the sky."

"Well, I did, but that was sort of a warning. I thought at the time you were trying to harm me. You know, the authorities think you've killed four people. What do you say to that?"

He hung his head. "Yes, but I had to."

"Why did you have to?"

"They told me to."

"Who?"

"The doctors."

"Which doctors, Philip?"

"At the place."

"From where you escaped?"

"Yes."

"But why would they want you to kill someone, especially four people?"

"I don't know."

I wondered if he was schizophrenic, considering those patients hear voices and hallucinate. That might account for his actions, which would be far better than him having acted upon the instruction of his caretakers from the Blue Lake Hospital, which would be a tough pill to swallow.

"I'm going home. Would you like a ride somewhere? From the looks of your shoes, you've been doing a lot of walking lately."

"Food?"

"Yes, we have food at home."

"Okay."

I unlocked the doors, and he leapt into the passenger seat. He applied his seat belt, and I called Mary Louise and told her of our visitor that was on the way. J. J. had picked up Junior and left for Dallas, for which we were both relieved.

Philip was silent on the way home but busied himself with turning various devices on the dashboard on and off like a child might, in essence discovering how they worked. He obviously had a degree of intelligence, but I was not qualified to determine to what extent. He didn't seem to be upset that he had killed four people, so perhaps whatever mental disorder he had might have affected his conscience.

After his exploration of the dashboard, he sat silently in his seat and didn't seem ill at ease without conversation. I, on the other hand, felt compelled to ask questions and make small talk.

"Do you remember your mother?"

"Yes. She was beautiful. She died."

"From what, do you know?"

"No. She had to take a lot of pills. She was happy sometimes, sometimes sad, sometimes wild. She was in the hospital when I was born. She used to tell me that I was special, and that the way I looked would scare people, but that was because of all the pills they made her take when I was in her tummy. But she always told me they didn't know I was growing in her tummy when they gave her all the pills."

That sounded to me like his mother was perhaps bipolar as well and was on meds, and she had been on some sort of toxic medication or medications during her first trimester that had affected the genetic structure of her child.

"So, you lived at the hospital for a while after you were born?"

"I lived there with Mommy."

"Do you have any idea about dates of when you were born, or when your Mommy died?"

"What are dates?"

"Like November the eleventh, 1983, for example."

He looked at me blankly, and it seemed to me he had no concept of the word "date." I would have to find another source for the timeline he had been describing. Sadness crept over me, with this young man sitting next to me whose life was filled with challenges from the day he was born.

When we arrived at home and I pulled into the garage, Philip bounded from the truck, hatchet in hand. Tip came to the inside garage door to greet me as always but stopped when he saw my guest. His greeting became a low growl. I was worried about the hatchet being used as a weapon against my dog, so I moved to Philip's right side and gently removed the weapon from his hand. I was careful to handle as little of the wooden end of the hatchet as possible, as more than likely prints would need to be recovered from the weapon.

"We do not allow hatchets in the house, Philip." I laid what was obviously his security blanket on a workbench. "You can pick up the hatchet later. By the way, the dog's name is Tip, and he wants to be your friend. Have you ever had a dog?" I asked, in an effort to distract him.

He shook his head, and he was wary. He let Tip come closer and smell him. Tip sniffed his jeans, his arms, his shoes. Philip thought that was funny and laughed with a croak that to him was a sign of happiness. He put his hand out, and bless his little doggie heart, Tip licked it. Philip patted Tip on the head, and Tip wagged his tail. And suddenly, all was fine between the two of them. And that reminded me that the word "dog" spelled backward is "god," and that we should never underestimate the healing power of animals.

Mary Louise was wary at the presence of Philip in our house. She was extraordinarily kind to him, though, and took him into the bathroom and cleaned him up. She found an old shirt of mine for him to wear while she put his dirty clothes into the washer. I wondered if he had worn underwear, but I declined to verbalize the question. Philip wandered the house, looking at this and that but touching nothing. I fixed Mary Louise and I a cocktail, then I sat at the bar and watched her prepare dinner.

"Jim, his spine is horrible. He has a long and severe curvature from his little shoulder blades down to his waist. Also, a curvature just below his neck. Want to tell me how this came about?"

"He probably has a congenital scoliosis and a kyphosis as well. Both are probably genetic and were present to some degree at birth. Both curves get worse over time without treatment."

"Jim, I'm asking how it came to pass that he is sitting in our kitchen."

I told her what had happened, and about our conversation on the way home.

"What do we do with him?"

"No idea. From what I can ascertain, he escaped from Blue Lake. I sense he's been living on the streets, but he's seen Shannon Wright; we know that because she admitted it. He has some degree of mental capacity, but it's doubtful his level would be high enough that he would be able to live on his own. We need to call Joan Wilcox for sure."

"And what will she do with a mentally disabled person? Probably call social services as well"

"Why don't we eat first, after which I'll place a call to Joan. Maybe we'll be smarter after dinner. Are we having smart food?"

I asked playfully. However, the look she gave me was indicative that to her, the situation was much more serious than it was to me. It was serious to me as well, but I don't like serious, so I usually cover that up with inane comments, which on this occasion Mary Louise did not appreciate.

Philip had obviously never been taught any table manners. He ate sloppily and ravenously, and with his fingers. Fortunately, Mary Louise had prepared fried chicken, which was meant to be eaten with one's fingers anyway. Tip was having a field day, scarfing Philip's leftovers off the floor. In his doggie mind, Junior had just left and was replaced by Philip, and all the extra food was making him happy, as his tail would not stop wagging.

I called Sheriff Joan after dinner, told her that her potential killer was in my house, and asked what she would suggest we do.

"I'll be there in half an hour. I'll get social services on my cell, and they can meet me there. You know we're obligated to take him into custody, don't you?"

"Yes," I sighed. "The entire scenario is just too sad, and I'm helpless to do anything about it."

"Jim, you've captured our only suspect in four murders. We have a duty to the families to get to the bottom of this serial killer business, and he is our best suspect, in fact our only suspect. You've done us all a great service."

Philip sat on the couch and looked through some of the books that Mary Louise had been reading Junior. When he read, he carefully mouthed the words, but silently. I couldn't tell if he could read or not. Mary Louise felt my concern, stepped over to the sofa, and sat next to Philip.

"Can you read me a story"? she asked him.

He looked at her with his unusual face and smiled a crooked smile. "Not so good," he said.

"Reading takes practice. Just do your best."

He started to read a few words, stumbled over many of them, but then got through three pages before our doorbell rang. He continued to sit next to Mary Louise and attempted to read while Joan Wilcox and a deputy entered the house. Behind them was a woman from Burnet County social services, accompanied by a male attendant who was present due to the gravity of the situation.

"Tell me you have the weapon," Joan said.

"On the workbench in the garage."

The deputy left the entry and retrieved the hatchet, returning with it wrapped in an evidence bag.

"Again, you know we have to take him. With his history, he might wake up in the night and stab you and Mary Louise to death. I cannot take that chance."

"I know, Joan, but it still feels like a sad state of affairs."

Joan and her three assistants approached the couch, and when Philip saw what was about to happen, he jumped up and ran toward the front door, which was ajar. The deputy grabbed him by the legs, which made Philip howl like he was caught in a bear trap. He began screaming and attempted to beat the officer away with his fists. Joan and the two folks from social services were finally able to subdue him and put him in handcuffs and a straitjacket. Philip continued to scream and bellow words I could not understand as they carried him out to the squad car. Mary Louise and I stood at the open front door and watched the squad car leave the driveway with its lights and siren on. Philip stared at us through the back window as the officers took him to yet another fate. Mary Louise cried, Tip barked, and I felt like I had accomplished the worst betrayal of my life.

CHAPTER 22

# LORENA AND PHILIP

The remainder of the work week passed by uneventfully. Tuesday office patients, Wednesday surgery, and Thursday office patients all went smoothly, without a hitch and with no surprises. There were no emergency admissions on Thursday, which allowed me to play in my Friday golf game with the Horseshoe Bay Bandits. I thought that playing golf would provide me with a respite from the angst I had about Philip's condition and his surroundings, but the nagging worry just would not go away. I had a lackluster performance on the Summit course and probably cost my teammates a few bucks. I offered half-heartedly to pay their antes for the game, but I had no takers. The one thing about golf that's consistent is that one's play is never consistent. I had a couple of beers with the fellows in the spirit of camaraderie, but my mood didn't improve.

Although it was late in the day, I took a chance and called Dr. William Watson at the Blue Lake Psychiatric Hospital in Austin. His assistant answered, told me to hold, then post haste put me through to the chief of psychiatry.

"What can I do for you, Dr. Brady?"

"Dr. Buck Owens sends his regards. He told me you had called him after my visit."

"Buck and I go back a long way. Don't get the wrong impression, Doctor, but—"

"Look, you didn't like my questions last week, and you won't like what I'm calling about today. Philip, last name unknown, was captured at my home Monday evening. He had somehow located my office and confronted me in the parking garage, he and his little hatchet friend. I was able to get him into the truck, both of us unharmed, and took him to my home. My wife cleaned him up and we fed him a meal. After, I called Sheriff Wilcox of Burnet County, and she arrived with a deputy and two members of the Social Services Department. It took all four of them to get him handcuffed, into a straitjacket, and into her squad car. And I feel terrible about it all."

"Philip needs to be returned to us. This is his home. We care for him here, we understand him, his needs are met. He cannot function in a normal capacity in society. He needs to be institutionalized permanently."

"What is his diagnosis? I mean, I understand severe scoliosis and kyphosis, and his facial differences, but what is his mental status? Is he bipolar, or schizophrenic, or does he have some other psychiatric label applied to him? He told me he killed four people, and I know the murders were methodical, in the same manner. He was able to track down his victims at locations other than their place of residence. And hell, he located me! He must have the mental acuity to accomplish all that."

"I'm unable to share his medical history with you, HIPPA rules being what they are. You're not family, or his treating physician. Honestly, you have no stake in the game at all."

"Here is what is going to happen, Dr. Watson. Philip is likely going to be charged with four counts of murder in the first degree, being as how they were not spontaneous acts but rather all premeditated. His life is going to become an open book. His mother's life is going to become public knowledge as well. The reporters and pundits and novel writers are going to have a field day trying to answer the question of how in the world a physically and mentally challenged young man living in a psychiatric institution became a serial killer. And that question will be asked of you what will seem like a million times. You can help yourself, and Philip, and the rest of the planet by cooperating, and the first step in that process will be to email Philip's medical records to me as soon as we get off the phone. If you choose not to take the high road, my next call will be to Assistant Special Agent in Charge of the Austin FBI Susan Beeson, who happens to be a friend of mine and with whom I have worked on many cases."

Watson was silent for a moment. "Can you assure me that Blue Lake and my staff will be placed in the most favorable light possible, and that you'll do your best to maintain the integrity of our reputation?"

"I will tell you this, Doctor. Send me the records, let me review them, and give me some time to evaluate what is in there. As a favor to you and your old friend Buck Owens, I will do my best to be objective. From the outside looking in, however, the situation does not look particularly good for either you or your hospital."

We hung up, and I headed for home. As I was pulling into the driveway, I heard a loud PING from my phone. Medical records, I hoped.

I opened a bottle of Rombauer chardonnay for Mary Louise and poured myself an eighteen-year-old Macallan scotch. We sat together in front of the computer in my office and opened the files Watson had sent me.

Philip Haskins was born twenty-seven years ago on the tenth of November at Blue Lake Hospital in Austin, Texas. His mother,

Lorena Haskins, was at the time an inpatient at Blue Lake. It was not clear from the records why the mother, once in labor, was not transferred to a general hospital or an OB-GYN facility for the birthing process. According to the notes I read, a team of specialists was brought into Blue Lake to accomplish the delivery. The only hint in the records was that Lorena was a severely unstable schizophrenic, and perhaps moving her to another facility was considered unsafe for her, the baby, and the treating medical personnel.

Lorena had been monitored during the prenatal period, and the doctors knew there was a problem with the fetus. Periodic ultrasounds and an amniocentesis during the second trimester showed fetal anomalies. Consideration was given to terminating the pregnancy, but there was the murky problem of parental consent. Because of her mental status, Lorena was not able to grant the doctors permission. She had been committed to Blue Lake by her mother years before and was essentially a ward of the state. Her mother had passed away and there was no clear chain of command in granting permission for the termination. That would have required involving the State Medical Board of Texas, and the legislature, so the doctors opted to allow the pregnancy to continue. There was also the issue of the causation of Philip's physical anomalies, and while antipsychotic medication given to her during the first trimester was purported to be the cause, that issue was glossed over. Also artfully ignored was the question of how Lorena had become pregnant in the first place, as she was an institutionalized mental patient.

The special team brought in for the delivery knew that a C-section would be required, so when Lorena went into labor, they were prepared. During the procedure, the medical team noted brown meconium stain, indicative of chronic fetal distress.

Because his mouth was irregular and his lungs underdeveloped, a breathing tube had to be inserted soon after delivery. His facial features were atypical, and his spine was barely compatible with sustaining life due to lung compression and restriction of air flow from severe scoliosis and kyphosis. But by some miracle, Philip survived.

Mother and child lived together at Blue Lake. She was unable to nurse, whether due to physical or mental reasons or perhaps both, but she was able to provide nourishment with a bottle several times a day. Eventually Philip was able to eat soft food, and he thrived. Philip's lungs improved, and although his condition affected his physical development, he eventually learned to walk. He was short in stature throughout his growth, but he was lightning-quick with his movements.

When Philip was five years old, a tragic event happened. Lorena, for undetermined reasons, tried to kill young Philip. While mother and child were allowed access to open areas of the hospital at certain times, they were more often confined to quarters. The nursing staff had heard screaming coming from behind their locked door, ran in, and found that Lorena had a choke hold on Philip, and he was drowning for lack of air. The staff were able to disentangle the two. Lorena was raging, screaming vile profanities at her son and exhibiting uncontrollable anger, and had to be sedated. The nurses all carried syringes of sedatives in their smocks for just such an occasion, being as Blue Lake was a psychiatric hospital and psychotic outbursts were not uncommon. But three of the nurses involved in the incident used their loaded syringes at the same time, which put Lorena out like a light. Unfortunately, she had received a triple dose of an anti-anxiety medication, and shortly thereafter quit breathing. Resuscitation attempts by the staff were instituted immediately, but Lorena expired. Even though she had attempted to murder her son, Philip loved his mother, and when he realized she was dead, he became wild and uncontrollable. He had to be sedated and restrained, and he remained so for several days.

"This is a horror story," said Mary Louise.

"Beyond that, even. I need another drink. You?"

"Please."

I refreshed our libations, and we continued to read the sad and sordid story of Philip Haskins, who never really had a chance in the world through no fault of his own.

Philip had fewer mental health issues than his mother, and although he exhibited mood swings, emotional outbursts, and depressive periods, he didn't receive a schizophrenic diagnosis from the doctors at Blue Lake. He didn't seem to hallucinate or hear voices, but he did experience manic and depressive episodes, so he was diagnosed as having bipolar disorder. The doctors experimented with several different medications, and ultimately his emotions became more balanced, and he seemed to settle into a routine. It was not clear how he managed to stay at Blue Lake. He had no parents and no other living relatives, as far as the medical records indicated. Was he a ward of the state, as had been his mother? That issue was not clearly addressed in the records, which amazed both Mary Louise and me. It was like the kid just disappeared from public existence.

He received some semblance of an education at his place of residence as he grew older. He had a learning disability, certainly, but he could learn. He socialized with the staff and other residents, as well as the part timers in for a ninety-day stay, and he became a fixture.

At some point in his childhood, he developed an intimate relationship with a staff psychiatrist. The doctor, by the name of Theo Strong, was interested in all things Philip, including his mother and her medical history. He did all sorts of tests on Philip: emotional, psychological, and physical. He went back through the medical records and researched the life of Lorena Haskins, and the route she had taken with her life that resulted in her being committed to the hospital on a permanent basis. In researching Lorena's history, the doctor discovered that one of the medications she was being given for her psychotic problems when she was pregnant early on was Equiliminbital. He had made notes in Lorena's chart that that drug had been developed by the laboratories at Blue Lake, and that while it was FDA approved, it had been taken off the market and then reinstated after changes were made to its chemical structure. There was no detailing the alterations in the medication written in the chart other than a notation that the revised drug was chemically akin to lithium.

The doctor experimented with changes in Philip's medication, which resulted in his heightened emotions and a trend to easily anger. The only reason given in the doctor's notes was that he was unsure of Philip's bipolar diagnosis and tried certain medications that were more specific to other psychiatric disorders. Philip began to distance himself from other people except the psychiatrist. The doctor left Blue Lake for a private practice position several years later, after which Philip fell into a deep depression. It was during this time that Shannon Wright had been admitted to Blue Lake, and they struck up a friendship. Philip's mood swings seemed to improve while Shannon was there, but he fell into another deep depression after she was discharged.

Then last year, in a fit of anger, Philip had accosted one of the male nurses who carried the keys, and Philip used those keys to extricate himself from Blue Lake. He beat an attendant into submission when he tried to stop Philip at the final security door. The attendant later died in ICU of a brain hemorrhage. When

Philip's room was searched for clues after his escape, the staff found a month's worth of his medication hidden in a sock.

"What do you think?" asked Mary Louise.

"I think the Blue Lake staff did everything wrong. Lorena should never have stayed there once she became pregnant. The source of her pregnancy should have been investigated, and she should have been transferred to another facility early on."

"Jim Bob, just where do you think a woman who carried a diagnosis of schizophrenia, was a ward of the state, and who happened most likely to be pregnant by a member of the hospital staff would go?"

"Well, how about the state hospital?"

"Let me think. Federal funding for state mental hospitals was eliminated in the late 1980s. Without adequate resources, I'll bet you that Blue Lake kept Lorena there because there was no place else for her to go. And as far as her delivery was concerned, what were they supposed to do? Throw her in the back of a car and drive over to Breckenridge Hospital, the city-county facility, and leave her with strangers? And what about her schizophrenic meds? Put them in a sack and give them to the first nurse they saw at the emergency room entrance? No, I think they did the only thing they could do. They kept her and brought the delivery team to her. Besides, none of his issues appear to have been a result of any missteps during the delivery."

"Wow. When you explain it like that, it does make sense. Pretty smart thinking, Mrs. Brady."

"And just to continue that line of thinking, once Philip had been delivered, what to do with him? Again, drop him off at Breckenridge and give the nurses a list of all his medical problems? No, I think that accepting the mother as a full-time resident at the hospital meant her baby would also be a full-time resident, especially when it turned out that he had a number of issues himself. As the old saying goes, in for a penny, in for a pound."

"What is your take on Dr. Theo Strong?"

"He seems to be involved in many aspects of this mystery. He was around Philip at Blue Lake for a time before he left for private practice. I could be mistaken, but if the timeline is correct, he was also on staff there during Philip's mother's commitment to the hospital prior to her becoming pregnant. He's been writing prescriptions for Equiliminbital for the four victims here in our area. And did you not tell me that a young man you operated on was also on that drug?"

"Yes, Matt Solis. He's still in HCMC, recovering from knee surgery for multiple fractures. He also has a bipolar disorder diagnosis, but to my knowledge, no attempts on his life have been made."

"I think Dr. Theo Strong deserves a visit, but rather than go it alone like you usually do, you should have Sheriff Wilcox present. If he is somehow involved in these misdeeds by Philip, you need an authority figure at the ready."

CHAPTER 23

# DR. STRONG

"**M**orning, Pops," said J. J. from his cell phone.

"Hey, son, what's going on?"

"Are you on the golf course?"

"No. Rain day."

"Huh. It's sunny here in Big D."

"Lucky for you. I thought I would catch up on paperwork, maybe take your mother to Austin for lunch and a movie. There's a sushi bar in Bee Cave that she's wild about."

"Good for you two. Listen, the reason I called is because I've done some research on Blue Lake Hospital—behind-the-scenes research, if you get my drift."

"I get that. That's been your forte since college. I remember the company you and Brad first put together, SETEC ASTRONOMY. You and he helped me solve the murder of our neighbor's child, Stevie Huntley."

"I remember the case well. Listen, what I'm going to tell you is proprietary information, and we'll keep our exchange verbal, no paperwork involved. Understand?"

"I do."

"While Blue Lake's primary focus seems to be the care and treatment of inpatient and outpatient psychiatric patients, they have a substantial drug development program. They have a state-of-the-art research facility and laboratory tucked away in the basement of their building, which, by the way, is owned jointly by all the physicians on staff. The way it works is that when the administration hires a new member of the group, they are an associate for five years. After that, with unanimous approval of the physician-owners, the new doctor becomes an owner as well, with a buy-in that comes from garnishing a portion of the individual's wages until the debt is paid. Once that process is complete, which takes about five more years, the new doctor is a full partner and shares not only in the patient revenue but the revenue from drug development. And that's when the mother lode comes in.

"Blue Lake develops new psychiatric medication, does clinical trials, gets FDA approval, and then markets and sells the patents to large pharmaceutical conglomerates for a lot of money. In some cases, Blue Lake participates in the actual drug distribution process by taking a percentage of drugs sold over time, at least until a generic is developed and approved. The patent for the original medication protects it for some years, which is beneficial to the bottom-line profits of Blue Lake because of the higher prices charged before the generic is able to be marketed."

"Why would that process, which I would call skimming, stop when generic drugs are developed?"

"Pop, it's not skimming. It's just doing business in a profitable manner. The reason the contract to share in the profits of distribution based on patient usage stops when the generic drug comes out is that there are virtually no generics created in the United States. While China has a booming generic drug business, the king of generics is India. Blue Lake apparently got burned once on the development of a drug where profits were shared with a generic company because the drug was recalled by the FDA. The generic drug had some changes made to it in the manufacturing process in India, which apparently is not uncommon, and when the FDA discovered the problem, changes had to be made to the drug chemically before it was put back on the market. Blue Lake had to pay a big fine, so after that situation was resolved, they stayed out of the generic business."

"What was the problem with the drug, or could you find out?"

"Severe birth defects occurred in the fetus when the drug was given in the first trimester. The name of the drug was—"

"Let me guess. Equiliminbital."

"Right on, brother. Would you like the name of the principal who was behind that drug's development?"

"Let me guess. Dr. Theo Strong."

"Pop, you're batting a thousand today."

I checked in with Belinda before we left for Austin. Ben Harper, whose hip fracture we had repaired, had been moved from the medical floor to rehab. Matt Solis had been discharged to his house, so we were devoid of inpatients in the hospital. Belinda was off for the weekend and had signed out to the on-call resident. She deserved some time off, considering how hard she worked. I bid her adieu and a pleasant weekend.

We had to drive slowly on Highway 71 due to the persistent rainfall and fog in low-lying areas. We arrived at the Galleria Mall only to find that the movie theater was closed for renovations. The Sushi Bar was open, so we went in and each ordered a Bloody Mary for our troubles.

"What?"

"I know you and I know that look," replied my bride. "Tell me you're NOT thinking of dropping by the offices of Dr. Theo Strong while we're here in Austin."

I felt my face redden. "I cannot say it had not crossed my mind."

She smiled. "I know you so well. We'll think about it while we eat."

Mary Louise was the sushi expert, so she ordered fresh dishes of salmon, yellowtail, and white tuna sushi, as well as a California roll and a caterpillar roll. For an appetizer she ordered edamame for herself and a spicy egg roll for me. She also ordered sake to complement our lunch.

We were quiet while enjoying our food. As the meal ended, Mary Louise again stared at me.

"What?"

"You're too curious for your own good. You've found yourself in difficult situations because of it. That said, there would be no harm in locating Dr. Strong's office for possible future visitations with Sheriff Wilcox."

"I agree. We would consider it sort of a training exercise, to save time later."

"Very well. We can drink some more hot tea to soak up the alcohol and explore on. I have rarely had the opportunity to accompany you on one of your excursions, so it could be fun. I draw the line at danger, however, so if it rears its ugly head, we are done and gone. Agreed?"

"Absolutely, Mary Louise. Exploration without confrontation, that's our plan."

The offices of Dr. Theo Strong were not that far from where we had lunch. The address was more Lakeway than it was Bee Cave, and the navigation system I was using indicated the building was located off Buffalo Gap Road. We found the address on a mailbox but could barely recognize a building behind a maze of oak and mesquite trees. We traveled up a driveway nearly hidden under a canopy of trees and wound our way up to the office site.

There were half a dozen parking spaces in a paved clearing, with steps leading up to a one-story building with a portico for patient drop-off. The structure was enveloped in beige limestone and was tastefully constructed.

"Make up a story," Mary Louise said.

"Huh? About what?"

"About why I'm walking up to the front door of this building and presenting myself to whomever greets me at the door."

"It's a Saturday, and I would expect the clinic to be closed anyway. However, if it's open, you could inquire as to their services, saying that we have a son in need of psychiatric consultation."

She looked at me for a moment. "That's a bit lame for an expert invader of privacy such as yourself."

I shrugged. "One cannot always be on one's A game."

She hesitated, got out of the truck, and sashayed up to the front door. I watched the shape of her hips as she strode and thought of all sorts of other ways to spend quality time with Mary Louise other than what we were doing. Nevertheless, I watched her present herself at the door of the clinic, then hesitate as though she were in conversation with someone, then motion to me to join her.

We stood in a small anteroom adjacent to a desk. The doors that led to the interior of the building were constructed of steel and appeared to be locked and bolted. The lady Mary Louise had spoken to was rummaging through a filing cabinet behind the desk and gathering papers.

"This is highly irregular, Mrs. Brady, showing up here unannounced, but since your husband is a physician, and a potential referring doctor, I'll do my best to accommodate you with all the information I have about Dr. Strong's practice and his patient base." She was a short woman, on the hefty side, wearing a long skirt and a billowy blouse. Her desk nameplate read Sarah.

"I was telling Sarah here about our oldest and his problems, and that we had heard about Dr. Strong from a friend. And that we happened to be in the area today and thought we would drop by and evaluate the facilities. And she's been kind enough to try and help us out," Mary Louise said, and winked at me while Sarah's back was still turned.

"As I was telling your wife, Dr. Strong's practice is mostly outpatient. If patients require hospitalization, he usually refers them to Blue Lake, where he was on the staff for many years. His specialty is behavior modification through drug therapy as well as psychotherapeutic techniques. He has a high success rate in stabilizing patients with mental illnesses. Let me see," she said, turning back to face us, "I have the patient evaluation forms, insurance forms, past medical and psychiatric history forms, history of Dr. Strong and the clinic, and a few testimonials thrown in. That should do it."

"You've been so kind, Sarah. We'll fill out the forms and get back to you. Jim, Sarah said it wouldn't be possible to see the inner facilities at this time. Another time, during the week, and in the presence of Dr. Strong, we would be welcome." She turned back to Sarah. "Again, thank you," Mary Louise said, and we strolled back to the truck. Sarah stood on the porch, waiting to see us leave. About that time, another car drove up the driveway and veered off onto an adjacent driveway. I assumed the car was headed for the staff parking lot, but it stopped abruptly, and the front driver's door opened and out stepped a medium-height stocky man with strawberry blond hair. He nodded, opened the trunk, gathered some papers, and resumed his drive.

We looked back at Sarah, and Mary Louise asked, "Was that the doctor?"

"Yes," she said.

# CHAPTER 24

# MATT

It's a rare occasion in the Hill Country when there are two days in a row of golf rainouts, but that's why I found myself in my home office on Saturday going through all the paperwork I had accumulated on the four murders of former Blue Lake patients. I made a list of facts and suppositions and questions that needed answers.

1. Hubert Brown, Delores White, Noni Berry, and Freddie Simons had all been murdered outside convenience stores via hatchet with resultant head wounds. All had been at Blue Lake at different times, all had bipolar disorder, and all were on Equiliminbital. That was the only treatment drug for Hubert and Delores, one of six for Noni, and one of four for Freddie.

2. Shannon Wright had been a patient at Blue Lake, was NOT on Equiliminbital, but had developed a relationship with Philip Haskins while they were both at Blue Lake which had continued to some degree after his escape.

3. Matt Solis, whom I had recently treated for a severe knee fracture, had served a stint at Blue Lake—I'd inquired of his mother when we spoke in the hospital—and was on Equiliminbital along with three other meds but had not been

in contact with Philip, as far as I knew. Was that because he somehow didn't fit the kill pattern, or had Philip not had time to carry out a murder mission on Matt because of his arrest?

4. Philip had been born at Blue Lake to Lorena, who had a diagnosis of schizophrenia and had been a permanent resident and ward of the state. Philip had bipolar disorder, as well as severe spinal and facial anomalies that occurred possibly because his mother was taking Equiliminbital during the first trimester of pregnancy. Who had been his father?

5. Philip had continued to live at Blue Lake after his mother's tragic death after trying to kill him. Was he not turned over to social services because of the checkered history of his birth at Blue Lake?

6. Mary Louise and I had seen Dr. Theo Strong, and his hair was exactly the color of Philip's. Could he possibly be Philip's father?

7. Dr. Strong had been at Blue Lake and was responsible for the development of Equiliminbital and had seen it through its generic conversion that had resulted in an FDA recall and fines. Did that result in his termination? Had he been part of the revenue-sharing arrangement between Blue Lake and the pharmaceutical company? The chemical structure of the drug had been altered during the conversion process to a generic, but that had occurred in India, according to the records.

8. Was there some relationship between Dr. Strong and Philip that was at the root of the murders, and if so, why?

9. All the patients on Equiliminbital had their prescriptions written by Dr. Theo Strong, while those with other medications had been refilled by another physician. Why was only Strong writing those prescriptions?

10. Did Philip have help orchestrating his escape from Blue Lake? And was someone on the outside helping him with travel between the murder locations? He could not possibly travel those spans without some sort of transportation, and without some knowledge of the sites where the victims had been murdered.

Compiling that list gave me a tremendous headache, which was relieved only by the preparation of lunch by Mary Louise. After I had a beer with my freshly constructed tuna salad sandwich, the cranial discomfort passed and my mood improved. In fact, I became a little frisky, and I asked Mary Louise if she had any interest in checking out the status of the outdoor hot tub constructed outside our bedroom behind a privacy wall. She thought about it briefly, then departed to freshen up. I turned up the heat to 90 degrees, left my clothes in a heap on the terrace, and climbed in the hot tub. She joined me shortly, fresh towels in hand, in the buff as well, and we proceeded to pleasure ourselves underwater in all the usual ways. Once we were satisfied, we dried each other off and headed to bed for an afternoon nap.

Once awake, I read over my list but still didn't know where to begin to find answers to my myriad questions. Mary Louise had expressed concern for Philip and how he was faring in jail. I thought I knew the answer to that question, but I called Sheriff Joan Wilcox to check on Philip's condition. I told her of my findings regarding Dr. Theo Strong, and that he might need to be questioned.

"I was just going to call you, Jim. I have news, but before I tell you, I want you to know that Philip Haskins is in one of my jail cells, and although he is not happy, he is in decent shape. The staff cleaned him up again and fed him. You know, I must admit that regardless of his history, he seems like he could be a sweet kid, in the right environment."

"I'll transmit those findings and opinions to Mary Louise. She's been worried."

"On a sad and very confusing note, another body was found this morning."

"What!? With Philip in jail? Same as the others?"

"Yes. Head wound compatible with a hatchet-like instrument, found under some boxes in the rear storage area of a convenience store in Kingsland. It's out of my jurisdiction, but I'm going to handle it because I have the other four cases."

"That does not seem possible with the presumed killer in jail. Have you checked for DNA matches on the hatchet recovered in my garage Friday night?"

"Yes. I got in touch with Dr. Jerry Reed at the coroner's office, and he took samples from our weapon and matched them to each of the victims. Now that we have another murder, I cannot say we have the murder weapon, only that our weapon contains the first four victims' DNA."

"This is unbelievable. Can I get the details on the identity of the victim so that I can perhaps evaluate whether or not there still exists the common thread of bipolar disorder and Equiliminbital as part of their drug regimen?"

"I can do better than that. Unfortunately, you know the victim. Matthew Solis?"

I thought my heart was going to stop. "Not my patient that just had knee surgery? Tell me that's wrong."

"His driver's license was missing, but he had other ID and he had one of those In Case of Emergency cards with a phone number. I called that number, and unfortunately his mother answered and just about had a breakdown on the phone. It turns out she had called local law enforcement last night and tried to file a missing persons case on her son, but it had not yet been the requisite seventy-two hours, so the duty officer told her it was too soon. He had a cast on his leg, and crutches nearby where the body was discovered. I asked her about it, and she told me you were his doctor and had performed surgery earlier in the week. I am so sorry. She told me you knew of his history of bipolar and his medication situation. Sounds like we have five for five victims with the same history, but unfortunately our presumed killer cannot have committed this crime, as he's been sitting in a jail cell since Friday night."

"What was Matt doing out of the house? He had a cast on and was on crutches, and still was in a good deal of pain."

"He got bored and went out with friends while his parents were having dinner at a neighbor's house. The boys went to a classmate's house for a teen party, and they got separated somehow, probably due to alcohol being involved. When it was time to leave, they couldn't find Matt, but they had to leave without him to get home before their curfew. The boys didn't want to get into trouble, but they did call Matt's mother on their way home, which is why she had called the station."

"I find it hard to believe his so-called friends left Matt behind."

"Well, it happens. The other boys didn't want to get into trouble with their parents, so they made a decision, which turned out to be a bad one."

I must have been white as a sheet, because when I exited my office, Mary Louise got up and ran to my side.

"Are you okay?"

"No. There has been another victim, this time a patient of mine whom I operated on last week. He happened to have been bipolar and was on the common medication all other victims have been on. This is hitting too close to home now. In all these investigations I've involved myself in over the years, this is the first time I can remember that someone this close to me has been a murder victim. You were almost a murder victim years ago, but I figured out the problem before the miscreant could do you in."

"And for that I am eternally grateful."

I felt my emotions let go, and I stood and cried while Mary Louise held me tightly. After a time, I was able to get myself under control, then felt the anger well up inside of me.

"I'm going to get the bastard, regardless of what it takes. I don't care whose toes I step on, or whose feelings I hurt; I'll find him and put him down where he belongs."

"Those are very strong words from a man who purports to be a healer of humanity."

"I am a healer, and a surgeon, but this has gone too far. This evil person has a motive, and I'll find out what it is and stop the process before he kills anyone else. It's time for Susan Beeson and the FBI to officially take over, probably something Sheriff Joan should have requested sooner. Susan might have been able to prevent Matt's death, who knows."

"You cannot blame yourself, Jim Bob, or second guess what you've done thus far in the case. Look at how much you've discovered. You made the connection between the bipolar victims, and found out that this drug . . . Equil . . ."

"Equiliminbital."

"Yes, the 'E' drug. You found it to be a common thread in the victims, and that they all had been patients at one time or another at Blue Lake Psychiatric Hospital. You mapped out the pattern, you just haven't yet found the motive. Now, you absolutely must be careful. I suspect the killer feels you're getting closer and will probably stop at nothing to continue their barrage of murders. I think if you can find out the why, you'll find out the who."

CHAPTER 25

# SAYONARA

Fortunately, it was Sunday, and both Mary Louise and I were too depressed about the killing of my young patient Matt Solis to get out and play golf. I had another full day off to act as detective and try to find a motive for the killer of five people via hatchet wounds to the head. The common thread was that each had been a patient at Blue Lake, and each had been taking the 'E' drug— Mary Louise's appropriate abbreviation—for bipolar disorder. What could the reason possibly be that those five patients needed, in the killer's mind, to die?

When Philip was the prime suspect, I had never considered motive. The complexity of his cranial neuronal connections was such that Joan, Susan, and I probably all thought that he was just unstable and had lashed out at his fellow psychiatric patients for reasons we would never understand. Now that another murder had been committed with Philip in jail, that opened the possibility that these crimes were somehow orchestrated for a reason by someone who had tried to cast the blame on Philip. Now that it was a fact that Philip could not have committed the murder of Matt Solis, we could take the approach that the first four murders were done by Philip, and the most recent a copycat killing. Or we could exclude Philip from responsibility for the first four and direct our attention to someone who was responsible for all five murders and who had tried to pin the blame on poor Philip but had lost his patsy when Matt Solis was murdered with Philip in jail.

But then who? And why? Did the murders have to do with money? I always believed in following the money trail. But money from what, and for what? Drugs? Patents? Something to do with Blue Lake and their finances? I found myself with more questions to add to my list rather than any concrete answers to the questions I had already raised on my list.

First, I called Susan Beeson.

"Calling me on a Sunday can never be a good thing."

"Sorry. I know it's your time off with the family, but I called to tell you that there was another murder, this time a high school kid I had operated on for an orthopedic injury."

"Same MO as the others?" Susan asked.

"Yes. He was killed Friday night, found covered with boxes at a convenience store in Kingsland early Saturday morning. Same type of head wound, and a missing driver's license. He was still in the hospital recovering from his surgery when he had a bipolar attack, manic in nature, and required a good deal of care to get him settled down. His mother had not informed us about his diagnosis, nor had she told us about his medications. He could have died in surgery due to incompatible anesthetic medication. She came clean after he was deemed all right, and we had a long conversation about his issues. He was on several meds, including the 'E' drug the others were on."

"I'm sorry to hear about that. I'm sure you're feeling the pain of loss, and probably thinking it was somehow your fault."

"Yes, of course I am. Mary Louise and I had a discussion about it, in which she tried to make me feel better, but you know how it is."

"Oh, how well I do. The request to get the FBI formally involved would have to come from Sheriff Joan Wilcox, but as soon as she calls me, I'll get to work on the case. I probably should have gotten officially involved earlier."

"I know, and I regret that you didn't. I thought the murders had been solved, once Philip was arrested and in jail, but turns out I was wrong. Dr. Jerry Reed matched DNA from each victim on the business end of Philip's hatchet, so the powers that be thought the case was solved. Not the 'why' of the case, mind you, but the orchestrator of the crime. Now, with another murder, we don't know what's really going on."

"So, now we need the motive, and once we figure that out, we'll work backward and find the killer, right?"

"Yes. Just to keep you informed, Mary Louise and I went to Austin Friday, had lunch at her favorite sushi bar, and decided to take a drive over to Dr. Theo Strong's office."

"Remind me who that is?"

"He's the shrink that's been writing the prescriptions for the 'E' drug that all five victims were taking. When I spoke with Matt Solis's mother when he was still in the hospital, she showed me his prescription bottles, which confirmed Dr. Strong had written her son's prescriptions for the 'E' drug, and another local psychiatrist for his other medications. That means three of the victims took other meds, but those were written by other psychiatrists. You need to find out why only Dr. Strong was able to write those 'E' prescriptions and not the other docs.

"Also, we caught a glimpse of the good doctor while we were gleaning information 'in order to help one of our loved ones,' a ruse which Mary Louise pulled off beautifully. The doctor has strawberry blond hair. Just like Philip's. The thought occurred to me that Dr. Strong had worked at Blue Lake, and that it might be possible that he is the unknown father to Philip, although that would imply that he, a staff psychiatrist, had sexual relations with the mother while she was hospitalized."

"And that might be a little far-fetched, Jim. Think of the implications and ramifications. But just say for the sake of argument that you're correct. What would that have to do with these murders?"

"Not a clue, Susan, but that's where you come in. I believe motive is the key to discovering the mystery here."

"With that I agree. I'll call the sheriff rather than wait for her to ask, and I'll invite myself to the party."

I took Tip for a long walk, through our entry gates, and down the hill toward the dog park and Lake LBJ. It was a beautiful Sunday afternoon. The leaves were starting to change, and I enjoyed the subtle reds and oranges of the leaves scattered amongst their green companions, still hanging on for dear life.

I needed to get my mind back on track to my real job, and I wondered about the schedule for the next day, Monday. I called Belinda on my cell phone.

"Sorry to bother you on a Sunday."

"Is everything okay, Doctor?"

"Oh, yes, I was just calling about tomorrow's surgery schedule, to see if I need to go in and review X-rays."

"Not really. We have five cases, three knees and two hips, and none are revisions, so the day should go smoothly. I think you can review the films before we start."

"Okay, thanks. See you in the morning."

Our walk back up the hill was disturbed by the insistent ringing of my cell phone. The screen indicated that Sheriff Joan Wilcox was calling me.

"Tell me there is not another murder, please."

"No, Jim, just a courtesy call to let you know that your friend ASAC Susan Beeson called me, and she is going to take over my case."

"Joan, don't you think it's time? There were four murders, now five, and Susan has extensive resources, much more than you have—hell, more than all the Highland Lakes police and sheriff's departments have, combined. I think you'd no longer be seen in a favorable light if another slaying happens on your watch."

She sighed loudly. "You're correct, Jim, that I know. We law enforcement types all hate to admit defeat over our inability to solve a crime, especially multiple crimes such as we have here. I'm just venting to a friend, truth be known."

Tip and I stopped at a rest area halfway up the hill. He was panting, so I shared my bottled water with him.

"I can't say I know how you feel, Joan, not being an official law enforcement person, but I feel attached to these people that have died, having reviewed their cases and spoken to their family members. This last murder, Matt Solis, has just about done me in, emotionally. I've given you all the information I've gleaned since you asked me to review the files regarding these murders. I'll be happy to share all the data with Susan as well. It's time for me to back away and get back to taking care of my patients. These murders have introduced too much sadness into my life. That's one of the reasons I went into orthopedics: there is little sickness and death in my business. And I like it that way."

"Well, I can understand that, friend. I'll officially let you off the hook. I'll put every spare detective I have on these cases, and we'll work closely with Susan Beeson and get this thing figured out. Your help has been invaluable. I cannot thank you enough for the insight you've given me in solving these cases. We'll take it from here."

And with that, I was back to being a not-so-humble orthopedic surgeon and dismissed from active duty as an investigator in the serial murder cases. I was relieved, or at least should have been relieved, at the freedom I suddenly had. I picked up the pace on our walk home, and I felt my burdens lighten as Tip and I made the last hundred yards of our trek to the house. As I approached the entry gate, I noticed that Tip was pulling hard on his leash in a direction opposite from home, and whimpering. I looked around too late to dodge it but saw a blunt object just before it impacted the left side of my skull. I felt intense pain in my temporal and parietal lobes, then saw stars, then nothing.

# CAPTIVE

I awoke with a splitting headache, and I reached up with my left hand to the side of my head and felt for blood. I expected to have a hatchet sticking out of my head, or at least a large hole in the temporal or parietal portion of my skull. There was blood, but not that much. I tried to probe the opposite side of my cranium with my right hand, but that hand and arm were restrained. I pulled hard, but a chain was attached to a metal wrist cuff and would not allow me to reach that far. Using my left hand to check the right side of my head, I felt no blood, or dents, for that matter.

My vision was somewhat blurry. I tried to focus on my surroundings and remember how I had been waylaid. I remembered Tip, and the walk, and his pulling away from the entry gate when I suffered the blow to the left side of my head. I felt around my body as best I could with my left hand and felt no other wounds. I still had on the shorts and sneakers I wore on our walk. I palpated my body, then both legs by flexing them up toward my chest, searching for injuries, but found nothing significant.

The concrete floor was cold, and I felt myself shiver. The room was dark except for a sliver of light shining through a window near the top of the ceiling. I tried to stand to see if I could reach the window, but the chain binding me to my wrist cuff prevented me from standing up completely. The chain was attached to a pipe of some sort, which was cold, so I couldn't tell if it was a functional pipe for transmission of water or not. I was able to stand nearly all the way up after jiggling the chain, but there was only three feet or so of play in my bindings, so trying to stand was wasted effort.

I sat back down, looked around my space, and deemed it to be a room around eight by ten. As my eyes adjusted to the darkness, I noted that the pipe I was affixed to was in the corner of the room, and one of several pipes; for what purpose, I could not tell. With the concrete floor and the pipes, I presumed I was in a basement storage room with a window built just below the ceiling. Yelling for help seemed pointless, so I ruminated about my current situation.

Who would want me captured and isolated? The serial killer? And why? Was I close to finding a motive for the murders? And was it someone I had interviewed? I was being silenced, at least temporarily, but I could not be silenced for long, because people would be looking for me. Mary Louise would leave no stone unturned in the process of locating me. Susan Beeson had the FBI at her beck and call, and Sheriff Joan Wilcox had local law enforcement at her disposal. I would be found eventually, but in what state? Dead? Not my preference, of course. I wondered how long it would take my friends to put the pieces of the puzzle together and find me before my fate was determined. After all, a person cannot just disappear into thin air. Some remnant had to be found, I reasoned, alive or dead.

My thoughts were interrupted by the sounds of a metal key in a metal lock. I looked around for a door but could not make one out, only what appeared to be a solid four walls. I tried to stand, then gave up. I was dehydrated and hypoglycemic, which, along with my head wound, was making me dizzy. I settled back down into my spot next to the pipes and waited for my captor to enter. I had not given up on escape, and depending on who came through the door, I would muster all my strength and attack.

"I bring food and water," said Philip Haskins to me, as he entered my cell through a door that blended into the wall such that it could barely be seen in the dim light.

I tried to control my anger and said, "Thank you, Philip. I was getting hungry and thirsty." He walked a few steps into the room, careful to stay far enough away that I could not grab him. He set a tray down on the floor, turned, and started to walk out.

"Why am I here, Philip? Why am I a prisoner? And what are you doing here?"

He stared at me like he didn't understand my words, then walked out. I heard the lock being turned, then silence. The tray contained two bottles of water, a sandwich, and a bag of chips. I devoured the food, then drank half of one bottle of water, not knowing when next I would be offered water. An adult can get by without food for ten to fourteen days, but water? Three days, then a fatal arrythmia would set in, due to lack of electrolytes. I had to conserve the water.

A little extra light seemed to come through the window; either that, or my eyes had further adjusted to the dark. I searched the tiny space for any useful object—a blanket, a weapon, a tool to extricate myself from bondage. There were some rags stuffed into a corner of the room. They were oily, indicating they had some use for the pipes that passed through on their way to a higher floor. I couldn't quite reach them, due to my restraints.

I looked at the nearby pipes closely and saw that there was one that ran from the floor to the ceiling that sat at an angle, while the other three or four were straight. I grabbed hold as best I could with my left hand and jiggled the pipe. It was loose at the top, implying its function was perhaps of historical use only. I was able to detach the pipe from its moorings near the ceiling, and then loosened it from its connection to the floor. The pipe was somehow stuck at the floor, and try as I might, I was able to bend it from its lower attachment but was unable to completely detach it. I propped it back as best I could so as not to attract attention. If I could break the pipe loose, I would have a weapon.

By then I was exhausted. I sat back down, leaned against the cluster of pipes, and fell asleep. I didn't know how long I was out, but when I awoke, the light from the window had faded, and the room was pitch black. I tried to stretch my extremities to keep them functional in case I needed to attack my captor or defend myself. I was already weakening after—what? Maybe a day in captivity, maybe, at the most, two? I continued my captive calisthenics despite the fatigue they induced, intending to keep my strength up and survive as best I could.

I heard the key rattle in the lock, but I feigned sleep, hoping to perhaps get the jump on my captor. Unfortunately, he steered clear of my path.

"Dr. Brady?" I heard Philip say. "Dr. Brady, I have food. Just like you gave me when I was hungry. I give you food, okay? Dr. Brady?"

He waited for a minute or so, then left and locked me in. I felt around the tray and found two more bottles of water, another sandwich, and a bag of chips. Since I was being fed and watered, I grew somewhat optimistic that I would survive the ordeal. After all, if it was the intent of my captor to kill me, why bother with providing me sustenance? Maybe they couldn't decide what to do with me and were delaying the inevitable. All I knew at the time was that I devoured the sandwich and chips, drank half of one bottle of water, and almost immediately was falling back asleep despite the searing pain in the side of my head. And then I remembered that I almost always carried ibuprofen in my pocket when I played golf and wondered if I had some in my walking shorts. By some miracle, I felt several of the small pills in the depth of my cargo shorts, pulled out two, swallowed them with a sip of water, and then dozed off.

I awoke to the rattling of the pipes, which sounded like water passing through. My partially detached pipe and future weapon was not leaking, which was a good sign. Light was coming through the window, so I assumed it was morning. I stood as best I could and relieved myself in the corner of the room, as far from my sleeping area as the chain would allow. I then suddenly became worried about the performance of other natural bodily functions, such as colonic activity, which set off a bit of panic. Which then encouraged me to try and detach the loose pipe, which I could then use to retrieve the oily rags in the opposite corner of my cell. I could use them for . . . well, for whatever need arose.

I tugged at the lower attachment of the pipe for what seemed an eternity and stopped only when I heard the key in the lock. Philip entered, sat the tray down in the middle of the room, and stared at me. I stared back, saying nothing. After a while, he turned and left and locked me in. I took a break, devoured the sandwich and chips, and drank half of one bottle of water again, building a stockpile in case the water deliveries stopped. Strength restored, I went back to the loose pipe and started moving it in a tight circle. I felt it begin to loosen, which prompted me to work harder, and finally I felt it give way from its earthly moorings. I fell backward from the force of extraction and caught myself before I landed on the concrete floor on the back of my skull. The last thing I needed at that moment was another head injury.

I inspected my prize. It was about eight feet long, with a nozzle-like attachment at either end. It was iron, or steel, and could pack a wallop. I was then armed, and while not battle-ready,

I was better off than I was prior to harvesting my weapon. While Philip had done me no harm, he was in league with whomever had, and he would suffer the consequences upon his next entry. I only could hope he had a key to my cuff and chain.

As best as I could tell, the pattern of Philip's visits was twice a day, once after the sun was up, the other at almost dark. I was not rid of the chain and cuff, but I had maneuvered the device such that I could almost stand to full height and was able to do some aerobic exercises. Push-ups and sit-ups were possible, as well as deep knee bends. I realized how out of shape I was and vowed to correct that if I was able to escape my captivity.

I tried in vain to avoid sleep to stay alert and at the ready for Philip's next visit. Unfortunately, his rattling of the key in the lock woke me from a deep sleep. I was somewhat disoriented and fumbled with my newly devised weapon, which I had hidden as best I could behind me. I didn't know if Philip saw the pipe, but during that visit he quickly came into my cell, deposited the tray in the middle of the room, and left immediately after without speaking. I didn't know how many more chances I had, but time was of the essence, and I felt I was getting closer to my fate.

I wondered why my captor had not shown their face, but that question was soon answered by yet another rattling of the key in the door lock. The room was dark, with only a small streak of light coming through the window, but there was enough light to see and recognize the man with the strawberry blond hair who Mary Louise and I had seen on our impromptu visit to Dr. Theo Strong's Austin office. He ambled into the room, moved the dinner tray away from me toward the opposite wall, and sat down on a small stool he carried with him.

"And how do you find your accommodations, Dr. Brady? Acceptable, I hope."

"What the hell do you think you're doing, holding me captive like this?" I said, with no small degree of anger. "I haven't done anything to you, and as a matter of fact, I don't even know you!"

"While that may be true, the way you're sticking your nose into my business leads me to believe that, left unchecked, it wouldn't be long before you have my plan figured out. And I just cannot let that happen. There is a great deal at stake here. You and your equally nosy wife saw me in the driveway at my office, so you've deduced that I am Dr. Theo Strong."

"Look man, I am but an orthopedic surgeon by trade. I am no detective. I have on occasion been involved in various mysteries of the medical type and have assisted law enforcement with investigations. But I can assure you that I have no idea what is going on with these serial murders. As a matter of fact, on Sunday afternoon while walking my dog, I had notified both the FBI and the Burnet County Sheriff's Department that I was pulling out of these cases and getting back to taking care of my normal business practices. And where is my dog?"

"Ah, yes. It seems he was so concerned about his owner that when I accosted you at the van, he scampered off into the wilds out of fear for his own safety. Some companion he was."

"What do you mean, WAS?"

"Just a figure of speech. I'm sure he wandered home when the coast was clear. Besides, you have much more serious concerns that the health of your dog. Your life is at stake."

"You better not have injured my dog, you—"

And with that, he jumped off his stool and slapped me so hard in the face that I toppled over from my sitting position onto the floor. He had on gloves, so the blow was not that painful, but he presented an intimidating figure, standing over me with an angry glare on his face.

"You're in no position to make threats, Dr. Brady. I clearly have the upper hand in these negotiations."

"Negotiations? About what?"

"I want to know how much you know, or think you know, so that I can determine whether you live or die. If I find that you don't want to share, I have some tools to aid me in my quest. Philip?"

As if on cue, Philip entered the room, pushing a small cart covered with a white sheet. Strong lifted the sheet and exposed what looked like surgical instruments, as well as an ancient machine for inducing electroconvulsive therapy.

"As you can see, Dr. Brady, I have tools to aid in our conversation, in case your memory lapses. I'm sure you recognize the ECT device, an old model but most a most effective device to create seizures and a loose tongue. And perhaps you may not be familiar with this tool," he said, as he lifted a long stainless tool with a blade on the end.

"This is an early instrument for completing a pre-fontal lobotomy. It's designed to be inserted thru the nostril, and through a sweeping motion, it detaches the frontal lobe from the rest of the brain. This renders the patient devoid of emotional entrapments as well as depleting most of the memory banks. It can be a successful procedure in the hands of a skilled operator such as yours truly.

"While I hope that I won't have to resort to these devices, rest assured I will not hesitate to use the tools at my disposal to glean whatever information you might have that I want."

I tried my best to ignore the pains in my abdomen that signaled one's bowels turning to water. I broke out in a cold sweat and shivered.

"What do you want to know?" I asked.

"Everything you know."

CHAPTER 27

# QUESTIONS AND ANSWERS

"**S**heriff Joan Wilcox asked me to investigate the first four murders: Hubert Brown, Delores White, Noni Berry, and Freddie Simons. I first discovered that each had had their driver's license stolen. Purely by accident I discovered that each of them had been a patient at Blue Lake Hospital, and each was treated for bipolar disorder. All four were on Equiliminbital, that being the sole drug of treatment for Hubert and Delores, one of five or six for Noni, and one of four for Freddie. Then I discovered that you were the prescribing doctor for each patient's Equiliminbital only, and other local psychiatrists had written prescriptions for their other psychiatric drugs. I thought that strange and could not figure out why that would be. That was the only connection I could make between you and the deceased patients.

"Then after Matt Solis, my patient, was killed, and I discovered he was also a bipolar patient and on Equiliminbital and other medications, I just wanted to run away, which is what prompted my call to the authorities, relieving myself of my presence in the investigation. That phone call was the last thing I remember before being accosted.

"At any rate, along the way I interviewed Dr. William Watson and Dr. Seth McIntyre at Blue Lake, and they finally released past medical records that revealed that Lorena Haskins, mother of Philip, was committed there, got pregnant there, and died there. After her death, Philip remained; whether he was a ward of the state or not for sure, I could not discover. At some point in time Philip escaped, during which he injured or killed an employee, according to Shannon Wright. I discovered Philip was a friend of Shannon's, who surprisingly had managed to remain safe during the time in which others with her same medical problems and same medications had been murdered, with the exception she was not on Equiliminbital. So, taking the 'E' drug seemed to be the common denominator in the slain victims.

"I also found through other sources—"

"What sources?" Strong asked.

I didn't want to invoke J. J.'s name or his firm. "Just other sources—online research and the like—about Blue Lake's patent program and revenue sharing with the doctors, but I could not put together a reasonable connection between that income stream and the murders. There was some data that suggested you might be the creator of the 'E' drug, and that perhaps an FDA recall put you at odds with the Blue Lake staff. And you might already know that Philip approached me on several occasions, wielding his hatchet and made threatening motions toward me. He also showed up at my home, where I provided him sustenance."

"And called the authorities," he interjected.

"Yes, because I felt he was a danger to my family. Since I have seen him several times during my imprisonment, I presume he escaped yet again."

"He is a slippery little fellow," Strong said, smiling. "Turns out you don't know all that much, only surface information, none of the nasty little details. Perhaps capturing and detaining you has been a waste of my time. I somehow thought you were smarter than that. Although the friend of yours, Susan Beeson of the FBI, she is a smart cookie, and probably could figure out the rest of the story, given a few more select pieces of the puzzle."

"How do you know ASAC Beeson?"

"I have not had the pleasure of her acquaintance and know only of her activities while keeping track of your efforts."

"And how could you be monitoring my activities?"

"Have you not heard of tracking devices and computer hacking, Doctor?"

With that, he stood and sighed heavily. "Philip, dear boy, please return our equipment to its normal place. We'll continue our discussions in the morning, Dr. Brady. I'm weary and must think about how best to continue. I bid you adieu until morn."

He and Philip then left the room. I heard the key turn in the lock, and footsteps fade away. I hastily scarfed down another sandwich and the bag of chips, drank half the water in the most recent bottle, and laid back against my bed of pipes to ponder my fate.

The metal-on-metal rattling of keys against lock awakened me with a start. It was a mystery how I was able to sleep so soundly on a concrete floor and a pillow of iron pipes. It was more than likely mental fatigue and fearful stress that caused my sound slumber.

"Rise and shine, Doctor," said Dr. Theo Strong, as he entered my cell once again. Philip followed closely behind him, and I was pleased to see the instrument tray was not present. However, he wielded a hatchet in his right hand.

"I've decided to give you a tour of the facilities," he said. He reached down, inserted a metal key into my metal cuffs, and unlocked me from my binding.

I rubbed my wrist and stood gingerly to my full height. After at least three days in captivity, my upper extremity muscles were stiff, as was my spine. I took a few seconds to stretch and to recover from my sudden dizziness, also from having been mostly seated for seventy-two hours. I realized too late that my treasured pipe weapon was left behind in the corner, and I almost reached for it.

"Leave the pipe, Brady. Philip saw from the first day that its position had changed, and he apprised me of the situation. He was careful to stay in the center of the room when he brought you food, and out of harm's way. He is very observant, young Philip. Despite his scoliotic and kyphotic issues and his orbital and maxillary anomalies, he has quite the intellect. And yes, I'm sure you've concluded that I am indeed his father, and you would be correct in that assumption. Do follow Philip out of the room," he said, and pulled a small revolver from his white lab coat and pointed it in my direction. "And don't make any sudden movements."

We walked out of my cell, down a narrow hallway, then up a flight of stairs, confirming I had been sequestered in a basement storage closet. The door we encountered was a heavy steel door, and probably rendered the basement room I had been in soundproof. The door led into a large room with high ceilings and many windows. It had been converted into a work area on one end, with tables, computer monitors, and electrical wiring snaked everywhere. On the other end was a residential space, with a full kitchen, a seating area in front of a massive flat-screened television, two sleeping spaces with beds, dressers, and stand-up mirrors, and a water closet open to the room.

"Walk that way," said Dr. Strong, as he pointed in the direction of one of the tables with several computer monitors. "Have a seat and enjoy the show."

He leaned around me, hit a few keys on the keyboard, and the screen sprang to life. I was distressed to see myself on the screen.

"What the hell . . .?" I asked.

"The magic of GPS using microscopic nano particles. I didn't invent the technology, but I have certainly perfected it. I took the liberty of injecting you upon your arrival, so you could see for yourself what it is that's so important about the research I have been doing for several years. I call it ITT, short for Internal Transponder Technology. Through this technology, you can be tracked all over the world with the simple injection of GPS-oriented nano particles. Can you imagine the benefits of knowing where every human being on the planet is at any given moment?"

"No, I cannot."

"Assume you wanted to start a war between China and Taiwan. You could selectively sequester an entire army, or just a battalion, and destroy those military forces with one well-targeted smart bomb. End of the war, with one shot, and no collateral damage to doctors, hospitals, schools, and the like. Destroy the military personnel, leave the infrastructure intact. And that's just an example of ITT's abilities. It has myriad uses."

"How did you go from being a prominent psychiatrist to developing nano technology?"

"Oh, Doctor, what is at the root of all issues? Money, of course. Let me tell you a brief story. I came to Blue Lake Psychiatric Hospital for post-graduate training in the field of bipolar disorder and schizophrenia. I was already a board-certified psychiatrist but was not ready to go out into the world and treat 'Joe Blow' and his bipolar behavior with little pills, day after day after day for the rest of my life. So, I applied for the fellowship and was accepted. I already knew about Blue Lake's little pharmaceutical scheme, and the massive amounts of revenue they were generating developing patents, and I wanted in on the deal. I figured that I would work hard, develop patents for Blue Lake, and cash in. But then came Lorena Haskins.

"Lorena was assigned to my care. She was a wild one, with about as bad a case of schizophrenia as I had ever seen. She heard voices and hallucinated, she was manic, then depressed. She was a psychiatric wonder. But she was also a looker. She would, after a year or so, come on to me on occasion. I knew that kind of relationship with a patient was strictly taboo, but after a while, I let my guard down. She had seduced me one late night, and while it was wonderful for me, she began taunting me with the idea that I had broken the rules with illicit sex.

"At the same time, I was working on a new antipsychotic drug, one which was designed to control the manic phases of bipolar disorder but not send the patient into a grave depression, which is why most of those patients were on several different meds. I was trying to achieve the goal of emotional control with ONE medication. I called it Equiliminbital, after the desire to 'equalize' the mood swings. It was a compound composed primarily of lithium, but I had experimented with moving the atoms around to achieve my desired effect. I had learned about the transmutation of lithium atoms back in grad school, where a savvy scientist had converted lithium into helium, the first known nuclear reaction. I experimented with my new drug in the lab, and clinical trials on mice through genetic engineering were successful, but I needed people to try it on.

"I talked the faculty at Blue Lake into letting me conduct a clinical trial on the 'E' drug. I put Lorena into the study, partly because she needed the medication, partly because I was angry at her for the constant taunting. She was making my life hell. Unfortunately, she got pregnant while on 'E.' Because she was a ward of the state, and due to her extreme psychiatric problems, staff decided to have her child delivered at Blue Lake. I suggested strongly that the pregnancy be terminated, but she was unable to give consent. Philip, as Lorena's offspring, became a ward of the state as well, so they lived together in residence at the hospital.

"Meanwhile, over the next few years, my new drug was working well, and 'E' was pre-approved by the FDA. I saw patents in my future, and scads of money, but the hospital executives became increasingly disenchanted with me because it became clear that I was the source of Lorena's pregnancy. That strawberry blond hair. And one of the doctors who had it in for me—Dr. William Watson was his name—initiated his own study involving giving the 'E' drug to mice in the first trimester. There was an unusually high number of birth defects like Philip's condition, and as a result, my patent was derailed. I was told that I would never be appointed a staff member, and that I would be dismissed at the end of the calendar year. And that since the 'E' drug had been developed at their institution, the future patent, if it became reality, would be retained by Blue Lake. However, the administration agreed to allow me to prescribe the drug, if it became approved by the FDA, and granted me a small pittance from the sale and/or marketing of the drug, should that occur in the future."

"You were still in training at Blue Lake when Lorena died?"

"Yes, and what a tragic day that was. Without a mother, Philip and I became much closer. It was difficult to leave him, but I was not able to care for a small child. I had to start my own psychiatric practice after I left Blue Lake and attempt to make a living, and I was able to succeed. It turned out that I had a knack with patients."

"Dr. Strong, it sounds to me that despite the tragedies that have occurred in your and Philip's lives, you've both overcome them. I'm having trouble understanding your potential involvement

in the murders in the Highland Lakes area. There is no proof
of your presence, or Philip's for that matter, at any of the five
locations where the victims were found. The fact that you've
kidnapped me speaks volumes about your participation, however.
Your mistake was in thinking I had figured out the whole story,
which I certainly had not. And even now, listening to your story,
it seems the only possible motive for your possible involvement is
a revenge element. The thing is, I don't think it can be proved. As
I see it, the only law broken that can be proven is my kidnapping.
And if you release me unharmed, you have minimal exposure to
prosecution, especially if I don't press charges. We could call it a
case of mistaken identity."

"Oh, Dr. Brady, I would love to see this situation resolved
in such a simple fashion, but unfortunately Philip and I did kill
those five people to see that the doctors at Blue Lake paid dearly
for their crimes against me. As a result, I cannot let you just waltz
out of here like nothing ever happened. I would, however, enjoy
sharing with you exactly how I was able to stage the murders.

"The key to my plan for retribution from Blue Lake was
quite simple. I had an exclusive contract to refill prescriptions
for recent inpatients at the hospital, an agreement I made with
the chief psychiatrist, Dr. William Watson. They were too busy
and important to refill their patients' medications, so they would
'farm out' mundane duties such as that to local psychiatrists. I,
however, had exclusive rights for refills on the 'E' drug, which I had
developed. I combined my ITT capabilities with my knowledge of
the chemical structure of 'E' and was able to insert nano tracking
particles into the recently discharged patients' refill prescriptions.
That was quite a feat of electrical and nuclear engineering, if I
do say so myself. I was able to monitor every move made by the

"Did it work? I mean, did your murdering of five people result in windfall profits for you?"

"Not yet, but we were in negotiations."

I looked at Strong like the horrifying anti-physician he was. "You killed five totally innocent and trusting patients in order to get a bump up in your finances. That is an act of heinous treachery."

"I'm extracting revenge on Blue Lake Hospital for cheating me out of my rightful distribution of the profits of a drug I invented! Me! Not them!"

I looked at Philip, then back at Strong. "And what about this young man? You slept with his mother. You put her in a clinical trial while she was pregnant with YOUR child, and he ended up with multiple anomalies due to your 'E' drug. Then, at some point in time, she had some sort of psychotic episode despite her medications, and she tried to kill Philip. And during efforts to save his life, she was accidentally overdosed on tranquilizers and died, leaving Philip motherless. And eventually, you walked away from him to start your own practice, leaving him in an institution with no parents. If you ask me, you might as well have killed Lorena yourself. The whole thing is your fault."

With that, he turned his pistol toward me. "Enough talk, Brady. You've heard my story, and you can take it to the grave with you."

As Strong lifted the revolver to end my days, Philip, who had been standing and listening to his father's ravings, moved in front of me, raised his hatchet and swung it with full force into the left side of Strong's head. At about that same moment, the revolver discharged, sending a bullet directly into Philip's chest. They both collapsed onto the floor. Philip was in agonal respirations, as it appeared that the bullet went through his heart or the aorta. I held his hand for a moment, watched him as he gurgled blood from the mouth and took his last breath. I then checked on Strong. He was a goner, the left half of his head caved in . . . just like his victims.

CHAPTER 28

# RESOLUTION

I sat in one of the lumbar-spine-friendly computer chairs and made one call on a landline phone that rested on the computer table. It was to Mary Louise. She shrieked with joy at the sound of my voice. Susan Beeson was with her, and they apparently started mobilizing the troops. She asked where I was, which I obviously did not know. I laid the phone down and walked toward the opposite end of the mammoth room. There was a door which led to a sidewalk, which led to another building I could see through the trees. I walked outside and breathed my first breath of fresh air in days. The living structure I had been held captive in was surrounded by trees and barely visible from the outdoors. I walked up the sidewalk and entered the front building through a simple rear entry door. There were examination rooms off to the side, and the smell of disinfectant permeated the air. I walked to the front of the structure, where I found a waiting room. To the folks seated there I must have been a gruesome sight. I was unshaven, filthy, smelly, and generally unkempt, wearing clothes I had not washed or changed in days. A young woman was seated at a desk.

She looked at me strangely, and probably thought I should be in an exam room.

"Sir, may I help you?" she asked.

"Where are we?"

"Sir?"

"I said, 'where are we?'"

"Marble Falls, Texas?"

"What's the address?"

She recited the address, which was not more than thirty minutes from my home.

"Is this Dr. Theo Strong's office?"

"Yes, one of them. The other is—"

"I know where the other office is. Call the police department and the sheriff's office. There are two dead bodies in the residential structure out back." With that comment, the waiting patients arose from their seats and all headed for the door.

I walked back out to the building where I had been held prisoner, picked up the phone, and recited the address to Mary Louise.

"Hold on, we're coming."

That sounded like a Sam and Dave song, and it was music to my ears.

I did not want to go back into the place of captivity, so I walked through the grass and trees and found my way to the front entry. A valet parker was busy bringing departing patients' cars. I stayed off to the side of the office building and tried to avoid scaring more people. Of course, it didn't really matter, since Strong was dead and his patients would have to find care elsewhere. I found a bench next to a fountain and sat, put my head in my hands, and in a very emotional moment, I wept. I heard the sirens before I saw the vehicles arrive, no later than a half-hour after I had called Mary Louise. I walked from my bench around the corner and headed toward the valet parking stand. Mary Louise saw me and came running. I was moving slowly from being cooped up—for how long, I didn't know yet. We embraced and had a brief tearful reunion.

"Tell me Tip is all right."

"He is fine. That's how I knew something was wrong. I could hear him barking from inside the house, and when I went out there, he was at the entry gate with his leash attached to his collar, but no Jim Bob. I called Susan first, then Joan Wilcox next. They put out an APB on you and gathered the troops, but had no luck in finding you."

"What day is it?" I asked.

"Wednesday. You were kidnapped on Sunday. Three nights and four days. It felt like an eternity to me. I am so sorry."

"Sorry for what?"

"That we couldn't find you. Where were you?"

"That residential building back there," I said, pointing, "has a basement storage room. I was chained to some pipes."

"Susan suspected the doctor, interviewed him twice at this very office. He gave her no clue whatsoever that you were being held hostage. She even searched that residence, I think. She could find nothing."

"The door that led to the basement was thick and heavy and probably soundproof. I never saw the point of yelling, so even if Susan was nearby, there was nothing to hear. Man, so close yet so far."

Susan came running next and hugged me rightly. "I am so sorry. I was in that building twice looking for you. I feel so stupid."

"That door to the basement was heavy and thick, and probably soundproof."

"I swear to you Jim, there was no door visible. It had to blend in with the wall perfectly. I just wonder if Strong had held other people in captivity down there, for nefarious reasons . . . behavioral research, maybe," pondered Susan.

"Quite frankly, Susan, I don't give a damn right now. I will leave the history of Dr. Strong and his victims to you and the other law enforcement personnel. And it turns out those two shrinks I interviewed at Blue Lake were aware of what Strong was doing. I can tell you all I know later. Right now, I want to enjoy being set free." I put my arm around Mary Louise and said, "Let's go home."

Tip was ecstatic to see me. He jumped in the air repeatedly, twirled his body around like a dancer, then fell, exhausted, onto my feet. He then jumped up again and repeated the routine. In time he settled down, assured that I was alive and well. I finally was able to sit down on a couch, after which he crawled into my lap like a puppy.

"Someone is glad to see you back," said Mary Louise. "He's moped around since you were taken, would not eat, would hardly go outside to do his business. He sat vigilant by the front door, waiting. I was sick with worry that your fate would be like the previous five murdered patients. Susan has been here since you disappeared Sunday night. She hasn't slept a wink. She brought in every spare agent she could find, searching for you. She's been in and out of Blue Lake, in and out of Dr. Strong's office in Austin and the one in Marble Falls. We could not believe you were sequestered in that residence behind his local office."

"I had no idea where I was, Mary Louise. The room was dark, with a high window on one wall. Philip brought me food on a tray twice per day, I think. He spoke to me only once, otherwise, he would put the tray down in the center of the room on each occasion and leave without speaking. I had loosened up a pipe that traversed the room from floor to ceiling and had finally detached it to use as a weapon. Strong surprised me this morning when he removed me from the cell and took me upstairs to show off his tracking system. I was sick that I had left the pipe behind, but as it turned out, I didn't need it.

"What I do desperately need is a shower," I said. I went into the bathroom, shut the door, and removed all my clothes. I planned to discard them, not wanting to leave any remembrances of my ordeal around the house. I stood under the hot water for a long time, lathered myself, and felt the tears building up again. I finally got out, toweled off, put on some clean clothes, and returned to civilization.

"J. J. has been calling. He's been beside himself. I called and told him you were safe, and just getting home, and would call him later today."

"I will. I need a drink. I know it's early, but it has been a long four days."

I poured myself an eighteen-year Macallan single-malt scotch and walked out to the terrace. Mary Louise joined me shortly with a glass of wine.

"Sorry, I forgot about you," I said, spying her glass.

"I can pour my own wine, silly. I am just so glad to have you returned safely. I had tried to prepare myself for the worst, but I just could not resign myself to it. I had hope beyond hope you would somehow be all right. And here you sit."

"There are so many ways the situation could have turned out for the worst. I'm thankful to be sitting here next to you and this one." Tip had followed us outside and sat close to me with his head in my lap. His stared at me with baleful eyes, and I so wished I could hear what he was thinking. But as I petted him, and watched him close his eyes in reverie, I decided actions speak louder than words, anyway.

Over the next few weeks, many newspaper articles and television specials chronicled the life of Dr. Theo Strong and his son, Philip Haskins. I agreed to one interview for each media outlet, figuring that was all I could stand. I gave the print interview to Del Andersen, owner and editor of our local newspaper *The Highlander*. She called it a scoop, because the big city papers had to go through Del to print the interview. The TV interview I gave to a local channel in Austin. It had been my impression that they reported the news in a fair and balanced fashion, and why not give the interview to the local news people. They worked just as hard as big-network reporters who covered the scene, and probably for a lot less money. Besides, they were nice people.

Our friend Bob Jackson was in alcohol rehab at Blue Lake at the time of all the "troubles." He survived his hospitalization and came out clean and sober. The staff did a good job of filtering the news, because Bob knew nothing about the deaths of Dr. Strong and his son, nor about the arrests of Drs. William Watson and Seth McIntyre. He was shocked to see the unedited newspapers and newscasts and wondered how such events could have happened right under his nose and he not know about it. He had great things to say about the staff in the section of the hospital where he had spent his time and felt grateful to be able to get his life back on track in the right direction.

Susan Beeson had taken great pleasure in arresting the two doctors who were complicit in Strong's scheme to garnish more revenue he felt he deserved from Blue Lake. Since my kidnapper and captor was dead, there was no one else to blame except the two principals. And although they didn't create the problem, they were certainly complicit in Strong's sequential killing of the patients on Equiliminbital. And once again, the crime was all about the money. Strong felt he had been cheated of his rightful place in the Blue Lake hierarchy and had lost millions in revenue from patents he had originated. The Blue Lake physicians didn't want to relinquish any of their revenue, and so Strong's plan was hatched to force their hand. And while Susan singled out Watson and McIntyre in the initial indictments, she didn't yet know the extent of the involvement of other physician partners. Time would tell.

I took off the rest of that week as well as the next week to clear my head and gather my wits about me. J. J. brought Junior down to see us because he wanted to see me in person to assure himself that I was going to be all right. He and I commiserated about the developments at Blue Lake while Mary Louise spent time with her grandson. They slept over for one night and were gone the next day. After the whirlwind visit, we sat on our terrace and shared a bottle of Rombauer chardonnay.

"How are you feeling?"

"Better every day, Mary Louise. I'm glad I took your advice and stayed away from work for the extra week. Emotionally I'm still a wreck, and best not to inflict my state of mind on the patients."

"They will all be there when you return, I'm sure. I realize those folks are having to wait an extra week or two and are suffering with their pain, but I think they would want their surgeon to be in tip-top shape when he replaces their bad hip or knee joint."

"As usual, you're right."

"I was afraid I had lost you this time, Jim Bob. Of all the times you've been injured, or chased, or threatened during these escapades of yours, this was the worst. You were kidnapped and held captive by a serial killer. The odds of your survival were low, I would think."

"You're correct. Had Strong not rehashed that business in front of Philip about his mother, I was probably doomed. Something snapped in Philip when he realized that his father was the reason that his mother was dead. And the odds of his simultaneous impaling of Strong with the hatchet and Strong's discharge of his weapon as Philip swung his weapon were infinitely small. Philip saved my life."

"I'm so sorry Philip's life was cut short. He had potential, you know."

"That's probably true, Mary Louise, but think of what Philip's life would have been like if he had survived. He murdered four people, though I expect he'd have excellent defenses. So where would he have ended up? Prison? Back at Blue Lake? We don't know if the hospital will even survive the scandal. And what other facility would take Philip as an inpatient, with his history? I don't want to think about it. I'm with you, sorry that his life was cut short, but . . . ah well."

We sat for a moment and watched the sun fade behind the horizon.

"I love you, Jim Bob Brady."

"And I love you, Mary Louise Brady."

"Welcome home, husband."

"And I am so glad to be back."

"I believe it is time to extricate yourself from chasing after bad guys, don't you Jim Bob?"

"Truer words were never spoken, Mary Louise."

We clinked our glasses and said, 'Cheers.'"

# ABOUT THE AUTHOR

**Dr. John Bishop** has led a triple life. This orthopedic surgeon and keyboard musician has combined two of his talents into a third, as the author of the beloved Doc Brady mystery series. Beyond applying his medical expertise at a relatable and comprehensible level, Dr. Bishop, through his fictional counterpart Doc Brady, also infuses his books with his love of Houston, Galveston, and the Texas Hill Country, but especially with his love for his adored wife. Bishop's talented Doc Brady is confident yet humble; brilliant, yet a genuinely nice and funny guy who happens to have a knack for solving medical mysteries. Above all, he is the doctor who will cure you of your blues and boredom. Step into his world with the Doc Brady series, and you'll be clamoring for more.

Printed in Great Britain
by Amazon

61458131R00133